RECENT BOOKS BY

Stephen A. Peterson

Profiles In Faith, Hope And Courage

On Eagle's Wings

Crossroads To Life And Living

Doesn't Anybody Want Me?

There's A New Kat At Scecina

Courage 360

America's Finest

Stephen A. Peterson

authorHOUSE®

AuthorHouse™
1663 Liberty Drive
Bloomington, IN 47403
www.authorhouse.com
Phone: 1-800-839-8640

This book is a work of non-fiction. Unless otherwise noted, the author and the publisher make no explicit guarantees as to the accuracy of the information contained in this book and in some cases, names of people and places have been altered to protect their privacy.

First published by AuthorHouse 12/7/2009

ISBN: 978-1-4389-8568-8 (sc)

Library of Congress Control Number: 2009911412

Printed in the United States of America
Bloomington, Indiana

This book is printed on acid-free paper.

Acknowledgment

I wish to express my deepest personal appreciation and thanks to Kenneth ("Kenny") S. Becker, Lieutenant Colonel, United States Army (Retired) whose record keeping prowess provided me with the 1970 Commissioning list of Second Lieutenants (our class) entered into this book.

Colonel Becker honorably and unselfishly gave 22 years of dedicated service to the American public and the United States Army in a variety of leadership positions retiring from active service in 1992. On behalf of myself and the great citizens of the United States, this grateful nation thanks you for your service. For he and all service members of the Armed Services make this nation the "Home of the Free because of their Bravery"

Dedication

This book was written to tell the stories of the bravery, sacrifices and truth about American service personnel serving in Iraq. Though these stories are about their service in Iraq, these are stories that may be told about the service of American military personnel worldwide. In order to protect their privacy and that of their families, these names and circumstances were altered. However, the good work and service were not.

The United States military has been unjustly attacked both at home and abroad for the mistakes and evildoing. Those who do wrongful acts and deeds should answer for their acts. The accusations of misconduct are extremely few, inexcusable and do not represent the conduct of the men and women of the United States military. The left leaning news media do not reflect the hundreds of schools, hospitals, roads and other public works American service members have built. It also does not reflect the fact that even in the worse days of the Iraqi conflict that 14 of the 18 Iraqi provinces were basically peaceful and its citizens knew peace for the first time in nearly two generations. Further, the left media never told of the American public the number of men, women and children who receive medical care (in the thousands) by American military and civilian medical personnel.

The good works and actions by those who performed them should also be told and represented more so. There is no doubt, however, that the vast majority of non-combat acts of United States military personnel express the true face of the United States and its people—service, kindness and love for the Iraqi people and people wherever the military is stationed.

What is patriotism? Ask too many people in the United States this question and one will receive a most confused response. The response here is to respect and defend free, responsible speech; To respect, support and defend the Constitution of the United States against ALL enemies foreign and domestic; To respect and defend every person's rights to life, liberty and the responsible pursuit of happiness; To respect and defend Godly laws designed for the common good for all persons regardless of age, national origins, ethnic group, racial group, gender and of peaceful religious conviction; To be informed; To participate in the educational, political and social processes of the United States; To actively oppose licentiousness and discriminatory law which attempt to destroy truth, justice, liberty and freedom.

Most service men and women know what price many have had to pay for freedom and the liberties so many flaunt and take for granted. They know that freedom has and never will be free. They know that each generation is called to sacrifice their time, talent, treasure and, increasingly, sacred honor and life that every American may be free. Those who believe otherwise will bargain these hard earned freedoms for despotism, terror and tyranny with the death of many!

For these men and women, the sight of the red, white and blue on the United States flag causes their hearts to pound. The sound of "God Bless America", "The Star Spangled Banner," "The Stars And Stripes Forever" to get the blood pumping, brings chills up and down their spine and tears to their eyes!

With that said, every American regardless of age, race, gender, origin and creed should be angered and incensed by those who call themselves "patriots" but fail to vote, fail to inform themselves regarding social and political issues, fail to question behaviors they know to be destructive and irresponsible, shirk their personal, familial, economic and social responsibilities in lieu of hedonism and irresponsible behavior and expect others to come to their rescue when things to not go their way.

Patriots are incensed by the excuse "I'm just a little person". There are not little people who are adults—just children! These service men and women have learned and know full well that there are people who do not want to be responsible for their lives, their liberties or be responsible for their happiness. They simply want to enjoy the fruits of the hard working people of this great republic but do not want to do the work required. They are the greedy who actively live off of or try to live off of the needy (the American taxpayer and service members).

This writer, the American service men and women who were born in the United States and the immigrants who made their way here legally are blessed. Many know it. Some do not! They have been fortunate to worship as they will, the freedom to disagree responsibly with the politicians and states-men and women, pastors and wealthy, to pursue happiness responsibly and to serve all their American and non-American brothers and sisters here in the land of the free because of these brave men and women who serve.

I also to dedicate this book to the 57 members of my Indiana University—Bloomington Army ROTC and to the 31 members of the Air Force ROTC class of 1970 who were commissioned Second Lieutenants into their respective services on June 8, 1970 for their dedicated, honorable and unselfish leadership to the citizen soldiers and airmen/women of the greatest citizens in the world—the American public. Leaders all, each of these men, put their lives on the line to sacrifice and give back to ALL Americans and to the world to protect freedom, liberty and the rule of law and common good of all foreign and domestic persons.

Army ROTC

Arthur F. ANDERS III

Angelo A. ARMONDO

Robert H. BAKER, Jr.

Felix M. BARKER II

Kenneth S. BECKER

Edward H. BINDLEY

Alan P. BLACKWELL

William D. BOYER

Arnold D. BRAY

Gary D. BROCK

Robert S. BUCHMAN

Edward T. BULLARD

Richard L. BYRUM

Michael C. CARNAHAN

Alan B. CURSON

Richard W. DAVIES

Thom L. DIXON

William W. DRUMMY

James E. EASTERDAY

John D. HENRY

Lawrence J. HILL

Anthony R. JONES

James D. KECKLEY

Randy J. KREIZENBECK

Roger K. LONG

Jay D. McQUEEN

Steven A. MILLER

Louden NAALE

John R. O'BRYAN

Gregory A. RIFNER

Alan C. ROSS

Richard T. SCHNAR

Robert S. SHAFFER

David A. SHAW

William H. SKELTON II

Anthony A. SMITH

Patrick F. SPRAGUE

Kevin W. SPARGER

William J. EGGERS

Thomas G. EICHENBERGER

Robert M. ELEY

Michael J. FEENEY

Robert J. GALKA

James G. GOGGINS

Michael V.GOVER

John L. HARLAN

Robert L. HARTLEY

Robert K. HENDERSON

Charles F. TAYLOR

William F. TEAL

David P. THOMPSON

Robert C. THOMPSON, Jr.

Malcolm J. TUESLEY, Jr.

Mark J.WEINER

William J. WILHELM

Denis L. WILLIAMS

Air Force ROTC

Gerard R. BECK
David W. BOLL
Philip A. CALLAHAN
James R.CLEMENTS
Mark D. COLE
Robert L. COX
David A. CRAIG
William L. CRAWFORD
Dale A. CUMMINS
Craig E. DAVIS
Jay L. DAVIS
Stephen H. DOWNS
Danny R. FOWLER
John D. GRAY
George S. GRUBER
Stephen E. JACKSON
Steven G. JOHNSON
Robert E. KAADE
Steven R. LINDLE
Jerome F. MILLER, Jr.
John E. MILLER
Norris R. MOON
Francis D. ODLE

Barry R. PEARL
Daniel H. SCHAUB
Donald O. SCHOOLCRAFT
Darrel D. SNIVELY
Lloyd B. THOMPSON, II
Victor I. THOMPSON
Kim M. WINTNER
John W. ZINK

I trust that the sixty plus stories contained in this book will inspire and inform you. You may rest assured that the vast majority of men and women in uniform represent you well. I encourage all who read these stories to thank them for their service at every opportunity. They will appreciate your recognition of their service more than you will ever know. Secondly, pray that men and women of the highest character will feel the desire to enter the branches of service and in each of their components—Active, Reserve and National Guard. Fight for your freedom and rights every day of your life. And never be afraid to tell wrongdoers the errors of their way and...You too will be one of America's finest!

Stephen A. Peterson, Author
Member
America's Finest

Table of Contents

Air Force

Be Not Afraid   4
Lonely Table   6
One Hot Summer   8
Magic Moments   12
The Prescription   14
Blessing In Disguise   16
An Attitude Of Gratitude   19
Making Burdens Light   21
Sergeant Mocha's New Car   23
The Reason   26

Army

A Soldier's Prayer   33
How Do You Say Good-Bye?   35
Onward Christian Soldiers!   39
An Angel In Uniform   41
Casting Stones Anyone?   43
Forgiving Yourself...Is It Possible?   45
Lieutenant Sunshine   47
A Bud Of Faith   49
Crossroads Of Life   52
Folly In The Workplace   55
In God We Trust...Or Not?   58
Meeting Challenges   60
Sergeant Mike   63
When A Soldier Says Goodbye   66
A Soldier's Tale   69

Making The Best Of A Rough Day 71
Suiting Up For Combat 73
When Forgiveness Really Counts 75
A Little Christmas Story 77
Somewhere Special 81
The Legend Robin Berg, United States Army 84
The Saga Of "Big Tony" 90
When Bombs Are Falling All Around 93
The Littlest Soldier 96
When There Is Love 99
Redemption 102

Marines

The Colonel 110
A Precious Gift 112
Starved? Thirsty? 114
The Little Iraqi Girl 116
You May Rest Assured 119
A Friend Indeed 121
Being Careful Of What You Wish For 123
From The Heart 125
Life Anyone? 127
A Special Little Visitor 129
Faith Re-Born 131
Good Samaritan Or Onlooker: Which Are You? 135
How Blessed We Are! 138
The Greatest Day 141
Mission Accomplishment 143
Fields Of Hope And Courage 145
Foolish Venture 148
The Promise 151
Gosh Something Sure Stinks! 153

Navy

I Am With You   158
Looking For The Good   160
The Important Things   162
In Due Time   164
The Conquest   166
Being A Blessed Receiver   168
Christian Or Not   170
Prayer Warrior   172
Hanging In There   174
His Plan For You   177
Proper Thanks   180
Best Counselor In The Navy   182

Air Force

The Air Force Song

The full lyrics of the song are as follows:

Off we go into the wild blue yonder,
Climbing high into the sun;
Here they come zooming to meet our thunder,
At 'em boys, Give 'er the gun!
Down we dive, spouting our flame from under,
Off with one hell of a roar!*
We live in fame or go down in flame.
Nothing'll stop the U.S. Air Force!

Minds of men fashioned a crate of thunder,
Sent it high into the blue;
Hands of men blasted the world asunder;
How they lived God only knew! (God only knew!)
Souls of men dreaming of skies to conquer
Gave us wings, ever to soar!
With scouts before and bombers galore.
Nothing'll stop the U.S. Air Force!

Here's a toast to the host
Of those who love the vastness of the sky,
To a friend we send a message of his brother men
who fly.
We drink to those who gave their all of old,

Then down we roar to score the rainbow's pot of gold.
A toast to the host of men we boast, the U.S. Air Force!

Off we go into the wild sky yonder,
Keep the wings level and true;
If you'd live to be a grey-haired wonder
Keep the nose out of the blue! (Out of the blue, boy!)
Flying men, guarding the nation's border,
We'll be there, followed by more!
In echelon we carry on.
Nothing can stop the U.S. Air Force!
Captain Robert MacArthur Crawford
United States Army Air Corps (now United States Air Force)

Be Not Afraid

Air Force Sergeant Michelle Gianelli sat alone in the Base Dining Facility while stationed in Iraq and heard service personnel at the table next to her talking about their Bible study class. She wanted to go over to them and say, "I overheard your conversation, and I just wanted you to know I'm a Christian, too." But instead of doing so Sergeant Gianelli held back. "Their discussion is really none of my business. They might take my intrusion as an insult to them. Besides, I don't know anybody at that table."

Later that day while taking a fifteen minute work break, Sergeant Gianelli overheard two Navy pilots in a light hearted discussion. One turned and asked the other amicably, "Say where are you from?"

"Grand Rapids," the second pilot responded.

"Grand Rapids!" the first exclaimed. "Hey a buddy of mine runs an automatic repair shop out there. Do you, by any chance, know Richie Chambers?"

"Know him! We went to school together and we've been friends ever since. You know, it's really a small world."

The two service members quickly became friends by discovering a mutual acquaintance even though they were thousands of miles from home.

Sergeant Gianelli, after being in two separate situations involving relationships, thought to herself, "the next time I overhear a Christian exchange, I will with the Lord's help, be not afraid to say, 'Do you know Jesus? Why I know Him, too!"

Lonely Table

During Air Force Basic Training, Airman Cody Fields was hesitant about saying grace while he was in the dining facility. Feeling that he might appear over pious, he tried to get away with barely bowed head and a quick "Lord Jesus, thanks for this meal. Amen." But a Basic Trainee Airwoman gave Cody a new perspective.

"I was really afraid my first day in the Air Force would be a disaster," she told Cody. "I didn't know anyone, and the thought of walking into that large Air Force dining facility and sitting down with complete strangers was just so terrifying. I almost got sick to my stomach worrying about. But while I stood in the line, trying to spot an empty table, I saw four Air Force Basic Trainees praying—two gals and two guys. Not making a scene about what they were doing, just sitting quietly offering thanks for what they were about to have for their evening meal. Right away I felt it would just be fine to sit with them. After all, we had a mutual friend—Jesus. So I went over and sat down. We began to talk. They really helped me get through my first four days of Basic Training and Basic Training in general. We all became real good friends after a week. And we also became prayer partners."

Regardless of where Airman Fields sat down to eat, he bowed his head in prayer before and after his meal just as he would do if he was at home. He learned that regardless of where he is it is appropriate to give thanks to God. And he came to know and understand that by his gesture he may very well identify some lonely Christians who may want to join him. In this way, they become friends through a mutual friend, Jesus Christ.

One Hot Summer

One hot summer afternoon in Iraq, Air Force Second Lieutenant Dennis Lewis was writing a letter at his unit's office. Through the open door, he saw a boy walking through the hangar accompanied by a Sergeant. His slow, shuffling walk drew Lieutenant Lewis' attention. He walked painfully seemingly concentrating on the ground before him.

About halfway through the hangar, he stopped and looked up. By his response, he seemed to have never been in such a large, spacious structure in his life.

"May I help you?" asked Lieutenant Lewis.

"Are you the boss?" the boy said in a low tone of voice.

"Well, I'm one of them but I'm not the big boss is that is what you mean," responded the Lieutenant. "But why are you here?"

"I'm looking for an American boss to ask for some food for my mother, sister and myself. We're hungry. My mother told me about Americans. She told me Americans are helpful and kind to people. My mother went to school in America. She taught me and my sister English. So we know English, too."

Lieutenant Lewis had been in Iraq long enough to know that people asking for help are very deferential, so the boy's aggressive demand puzzled him. As he went closer to the boy and the Sergeant, he could see a shinny object around the boy's neck. It was a medal.

"What's this young man? And where did you get this medal?" questioned Lieutenant Lewis.

"My family is Caldean Christians. My family has been in this area a long time. We have suffered much. My father and a brother are dead. They died because of Saddam Hussein. So I work to get food and help for my family. I work when I can sell the things my mother and sister make. They cannot do the things I can do because Iraqi society does not permit women to do these things."

Lieutenant Lewis and the boy stared at each other. It had occurred to him that it was the first time he had ever met any one in Iraq who had not been Islamic. The Lieutenant was probably the first American officer he had ever met in his young life.

So Lieutenant Lewis invited him in. He shuffled toward the Lieutenant's office door and stopped.

"Are you sure about this, sir?" responded the Sergeant.

"Yes, I think we'll be okay. He looked innocent. Did you check him out?"

"Yes, I did, sir. He had nothing on him except that medal around his neck."

"When we're finished I'll call for you, okay Sergeant. Thanks!"

"Yes, sir." as he left the Lieutenant and the boy.

"Come on young man. I'll get you some food to give to your mother and sister. What would you like to have? I'm pretty certain I could give you enough food for a least a week. I'll call my boss and tell him what I'm doing."

"You would do that for me?" queried the boy.

"Yes, come on in young man."

Slowly his eyes went down to his feet. Then he looked the Lieutenant in the eyes. "One of my feet was cut off by Saddam's men and can't walk very well. I smell bad. I'll make your place smell bad."

"Well, so do I," responded Lieutenant Lewis. "Now come on into my office so I can take you on down to our food storage area. I've already gotten the okay from my wing commander to give the food I requested."

Lieutenant Lewis and young boy chatted for another thirty minutes or so. He got to know the boy and his family better. He asked the Lieutenant if he was a Christian and had brothers and sisters. The Lieutenant responded "Yes" to both questions. He told the Lieutenant that he was the first American he had met that was so similar to his family in so many ways.

The boy's mother was an English teacher as well as a Christian who had suffered persecution for both. Though an educated teacher she could not teach because she was a woman. Likewise, the boy suffered for being able to speak English and even more for being a Christian in an Islamic country. And in the mind of Lieutenant Lewis, this soon to be 13 year old, was such a polite and gentle person.

Eventually, he prepared to go back to his family with 10 days of food. The Lieutenant reached into his pocket and offered him some money. Suddenly and unexpectedly, the boy became very angry, it seemed.

"Please, American, don't insult me or my family," he said in a low tone of voice.

Lieutenant Lewis apologized profusely. "I didn't mean to insult you or your family."

He soon became calm. "I came to this place as an outcast and a beggar. But you given me hope, dignity and made me feel like a man. Thank you American, Christian, man."

Magic Moments

Air Force Sergeant Kendal Adams slid into the front seat of his wing commander's military vehicle to drive him to the runway and almost knocked a little book to the floor. As he grabbed for it, he saw it was a Bible—even in far away Iraq.

"Sergeant, I use that whenever I'm delayed for whatever reason. Like having to wait for repairs to my plane or if the command orders us to stand by," the commander said. "I used to sit around angry at somebody or something if I was held up for any reason. Then, after talking to the chaplain, he got me to realize that any down time I had could be made a part of my day's worship time. I never thought of my free time or down time as a period I could use to worship the Lord. Any down time I found I could use during non-military activities as well. I can get a short prayer in while I'm waiting for a traffic light to change or when I'm out shopping with the wife and children. I've learned this time can be very rewarding."

Sergeant Adams began following his commander's example. It became so rewarding that he made it a real challenge to find different opportunities for what the Sergeant called: "my mini devotional periods". While cleaning his computer screen; waiting in line for a meal; even waiting in base headquarters to transport his wing commander became opportunities to recite familiar Scripture verses or to memorize new ones. They became periods for singing hymns or lifting up thankful thoughts to the Father for all of the thing he had been given in life.

Sergeant Adams, at the end of virtually every day, came to realize his blessings and how much time he spent with God each day. He referred to them as—Magic Moments

The Prescription

Air Force Major Brian Whitehorse, a physician, nearly ran through the hospital on his way to visit Abdulrahman A. Abdulrahman—an Iraqi he befriended while serving as a medical doctor in Baghdad. Mr. Abdulrahman was not doing very well following his hip replacement surgery a month earlier. There was talk among the medical team that Mr. Abdulrahman may never walk again on his on.

When Major Whitehorse arrived at his room, he found it empty. He was informed that he had gone to physical therapy. As the Major waited, he noticed a hand written 3 X 5 card taped to the medical table next to Mr. Abdulrahman's bed. On the card was written:

Three times daily—

1. Yield yourself to the healing power of Almighty God.

2. Imagine yourself walking even though it is painful.

3. Never listen to naysayers or anything negative.

4. Be cheerful and kind to all who visit you.

5. Give thanks to Almighty God for He is
    Good.

On his return, Major Whitehorse asked him
about his list.

"Dr. Whitehorse, you gave me a list of
everything I needed to do to get better and
be able to walk again," he said with a big smile
on his face. "That is a medical explanation and
prescription for getting better. But your list left a
few things out. Besides a medical list, one needs
a spiritual list as well. We Iraqis rely on the
power of God to heal as when we hurt. We know
His power." Within two months, Mr. Abdulrahman
was walking well with the assistance of a cane.
In roughly a year the cane was gone as well.

Mr. Abdulrahman went on to do very well.
No one would have ever thought that he had
hip replacement surgery unless they were told
of it. His comments reminded Major Whitehorse
how intertwined the mind, body and spirit
actually are and how deeply they truly affect
one another. Since meeting Mr. Abdulrahman,
Major Whitehorse, with his permission, made
up a copy of his prescription for good medical
healing in his office and in his heart and mind.

Blessing In Disguise

While serving on duty in Northern Iraq, Air Force Captain Justin Coughlin asked an Iraqi merchant how he was doing following the Saddam Hussein government. The merchant replied: "Everything is doing well and business is just well, too! Sure, I have a missing finger, had to rebuild my house now for the fourth time; and had one of my sons killed by Saddam. But I am not blaming God for what I have gone through. In spite of my losses, God has given me much—my life, good health and much, much more! God has even given me the opportunity to know freedom through the efforts of the American government and the kindness of those sent to free my country."

The upbeat response of the Iraqi merchant caused Captain Coughlin to raise a question: "What comes first in the life of people who lead contented, happy lives?" He thought happy people are happy first then developed a sense of gratefulness as a result of being happy. After meeting the Iraqi merchant, Captain Coughlin came to believe that people are happy because they are grateful for what God has given that person on any given day, at any given moment.

The Iraqi merchant helped Captain Coughlin developed a better understanding of gratitude and happiness. Within a matter of days, the man Captain Coughlin drew up a list of some of the blessings he had received. He started with what he considered as the ten most obvious ones:

1. sight
2. a job
3. life
4. parents
5. wife
6. children
7. freedom
8. good health
9. good food
10. a place to live

To further help him recognize God's blessings, Captain Coughlin developed a list of blessings beginning with the first letter of his name—C:

1. chairs
2. cheese
3. coffee
4. crackers
5. candles
6. chili
7. chips
8. chocolate
9. candy
10. cups
11. cereal
12. cellular telephone

Within a month while in Iraq, Captain Coughlin developed a list of more than eight dozen blessings he had received from God just using the letters of his family name. Regardless of where he was or what he was doing, he realized he had received abundant blessings from God—and learned the true meaning of happiness.

An Attitude Of Gratitude

While on military duty in Iraq, Air Force Chaplain Albert Michaels did everything he could to comfort the service members that attended his Sunday morning service on hot June day.

Chaplain Michaels delivered an unusual sermon on the subject of gratitude. That is, the importance of giving "thanks" to Almighty God for everything that happens to come their way. "For finding praise, happiness and joy even when there is evil, death and personal frustration can actually be periods when God's blessings can be revealed and manifested," said the Chaplain.

Upon completion of his sermon, Chaplain Michaels sent a small basket around for the assembled service members to contribute. When the little basket came back, there were just thirty-three one dollar bills and maybe a handful of change. In spite of the meager contributions, the chaplain raised his eyes and hands heavenward and prayed: "I thank you, Lord, for what has been received. For I know, Lord, that these airmen and women, marines, soldiers and sailor gave what they had to Iraqi children, your children, during the course of this day. Continue to bless these service men and women whose hands, through Your Most Holy Will, have rebuilt and built schools, hospitals, roads and homes for a people yearning to be free."

What is the meaning and significance of this tale from the front? It is two fold. First, that America's face is being represented well in Iraq by its young military men and women in spite of the extremely poor American media coverage of the full story of the American presence in a country that has know nothing but captivity and terror for more than thirty years. Second, sometimes when things do not go the way one expects them to, recall the chaplain's experience and thoughtfulness for what was received than complain. For God is in control and will provide what is needed in due time—not when humankind thinks it is time.

In this regard, many Christians recall the words of the Apostle Paul's letter to the Romans where he writes: "Eternal life to those who by patient continuance in doing good... But to those who are self-seeking and do not obey the truth but obey unrighteousness—indignation and wrath." (Romans 2:7-8).

Making Burdens Light

As she traveled on her first tour to Iraq, Air Force Sergeant Karen Krug confided her concerns to her dormitory mate, Sergeant Debra Austin. "I've discovered that I have been driven by fear for nearly three months. So what I've decided to do is to fast. No, I'm not going to give up food and liquid. I'm going to give up fear instead."

Sergeant Krug's concept fascinated Sergeant Austin. She never thought of fasting as anything but giving up eating. While in route to their overseas duty station, Sergeant Austin found in Isaiah 58 that God did not mean for his people to only refrain from food, but to change their behavior. She then came to understand what Sergeant Krug had learned through her Biblical reading and study. Because she too had fears about her deployment to Iraq, Sergeant Austin decided to adopt Sergeant Krug's fast plan as well.

Sergeant Austin could not recognize all of her anxieties, so she chose four fears she knew caused her the greatest stress. Then she wrote in her personal diary a pledge. "Almighty God, on this day I will worry not about being in Iraq, or about if I'll be able to go to college, or about having enough money or about leaving my parents, brothers and sister behind."

After reading her pledge daily for roughly three weeks, Sergeant Austin slowly began giving her fears to God. She noticed that as she began to confide more in God even her small often nagging fears began to disappear. Life without worry seemed to give Sergeant Austin more energy and she was more at ease with everyone around her. Her peers found her to be more helpful as did her commander. In her off duty hours she was able to complete online college courses. She was able to complete 24 hours of college work before she left Iraq. Upon her completion of her overseas duty, Sergeant Austin was able to save more than $7,000. Sergeant Austin was able to interact with her family on her computer website generally two times a week.

Sergeant Krug's idea for fasting helped Sergeant Austin remember that no matter how stressful situations may seem, God is ready and able to remove burdensome fears and the stress life brings with living.

Like Sergeant Austin, God is waiting to bless those who submit their fears and stresses to Him.

Sergeant Mocha's New Car

Following a 20 month tour of duty in Iraq, Air Force Sergeant Roger Mocha was granted a month of rest and relaxation in Kuwait before shipping out to return to the United States. While taking a tour of Kuwait City, Sergeant Mocha came across an auto dealership. He could hardly believe his eyes when he found a 2007 Toyota for just over $1500 and under 20,000 miles. The car was mechanically sound, the tires had good tread, the seats and carpet look almost brand new. The outside of the vehicle looked unkept and dusty. When the Sergeant examined the silver surface he could see dents, dings and scratches from its front to rear.

As the Kuwaiti salesman attempted to explain all of the good points of the vehicle, Sergeant wondered if the car he considered purchasing could ever regain its original finish and luster. Sergeant Mocha decided to do one more walk around before he invested his hard earned money in this vehicle. Taking out a clean handkerchief, he dipped it in a small amount of vehicle cleaner. On the worst spot he could find, he applied the cleaner. Much to Sergeant Mocha's surprise and delight and with a great deal of hard rubbing, he found that the dirty, dull, silver, Toyota could produce a magnificent shine. The salesman did not have to say another word. Sergeant Mocha took out his wallet then gave the salesman $2000 in cash much to the

23

salesman's delight. He drove off the lot confident that he made a prudent and wise purchase!

Christians in and outside of the Armed Services of the United States have the potential to convey the goodness, value and joy of Christianity and the Life of Christ anywhere he or she may go without a hard sell much in the same way the Kuwaiti salesman did in the case of Sergeant Mocha. So why do so many of the Christian faith often meet up with non-believer resistance. Fulton J. Sheen, a prominent Roman Catholic bishop of the middle twentieth century, observed: "one of the greatest sins of Christianity down through the ages since Jesus has been the sins of Christians that have stained the beautiful words and character of Jesus in the Christian and non-Christian worlds."

As with Sergeant Mocha's car, sin has marred and left stains upon our Christian personalities and filth that needs to be removed in order for the true beauty of the personality of Jesus Christ may be seen in us and eventually in the eyes of world.

The part of Christianity that many Christians do not like is the change that must occur in life through the buffing of brokenness, difficulties, trials, pain and suffering. For it has been through difficulties and the pressures of life that the filth and grime of rebellion and selfishness are loosened and washes away from human personalities in Christ. Paul the Apostle in his letter to the Roman's wrote that trials and tribulations produce perseverance, character, hope and confidence by the Holy Spirit.

Humanness generally desires a quick, speedy car wash to do the trick to deal with human sin natures. However, there is no substitute for the trials that can bring out the shine and brilliance of Christ's personality in those willing to accept His challenge faithfully knowing that He knows exactly what He is doing. It is up to the Christian to believe and trust is the most difficult part of the equation.

The Reason

Air Force Captain Rodney Ricks' plane landed at John F. Kennedy International Airport at 6:00 AM after serving as a serving as a surgeon for 19 months in Iraq. With a little bit of luck, he thought, he might rest up at an airport hotel before making a connecting flight that would fly him back to Tulsa, Oklahoma.

Within minutes after landing, Captain Ricks learned from a member of the flight crew that a flight into Tulsa was made available as a result of a cancellation. He decided to take the flight. Now he could be home sooner. He could be with his wife, children and friends before he had planned to be. Great! As he completed a fast jog from one section of the airport to another and about to board the plane, a baggage handler grabbed his duffle bag and threw it on a transport vehicle headed towards the plane. "Come on soldier," he shouted, "we're ready to go. Hubba! Hubba!"

As luck would have it, Captain Ricks was assigned a seat next to a teenage girl to Tulsa as well. "It's my first trip without my parents. Where are you going, soldier?"

"I'm sorry but I'm not a soldier. I'm really an Airman. I'm in the Air Force," Captain Ricks said smiling. "I'm headed home to be with my wife and children following military duty in Iraq."

"Oh, okay," she responded.

The plane shortly lifted off of the ground. New York City seemed to disappear from the clouds that seemed to cover the city landscapes. "I'm sorry Mr. Air Force person and I don't want to seem rude but I'm scared. I'm going back to Oklahoma to be picked up by relatives to be taken to the M. D. Anderson treatment hospital in Texas. I have cancer. They don't know if it's bad or not."

Though he was very tired, Captain Ricks didn't think that getting some rest before arriving in Tulsa was all that important at that moment. He turned his head to see a frightened young teenage girl holding tight onto a seat arm rest.

"Please, don't be afraid. And don't give up hope," he urged her.

Still shaking, the teenager turned her head and looked into Captain Ricks' eyes. Almost instantly, the fearful girl stopped shaking. "Would you please pray for me?" she asked.

"You bet! I most certainly will. I promise." She reached over the arm rest and squeezed Captain Ricks' hand. "Thank you so much!" as a tear flowed from her eyes. She then fell asleep until the plane landed in Tulsa.

"We're in Tulsa, Air Force guys! I'm sorry I didn't even ask you your name," she said now smiling.

"Captain Ricks," point to his name tag on his blue Air Force uniform.

"And your name ma'am?"

"My name is Sharon, Sharon Pearson. I hope you're not angry with me 'cause I bothered you during the flight. I was just so scared. But when you talked to me, my fear seemed to go away. It was like God made you say the words I needed to hear."

"If what I said affected you positively, I sure God did do so. He does those things. Now may the Lord bless you and help you through this difficult time in your life and be with you all the days of your life!" Captain Ricks said with a confident smile.

As he de-planed, Captain Ricks thought to himself: "I probably would have been angry. But her terrified look changed my heart and response to her. Now I know I was put on that particular flight for a reason. That scared teen was the reason. Thanks, Lord for a chance to serve you one more time!"

Army

Army Song

The Army Goes Rolling Along (1956, current official version)
typically only the first verse and refrain are sung (not including the intro)

Intro:
> March along, sing our song, with the Army of the free
> Count the brave, count the true, who have fought to victory
> We're the Army and proud of our name
> We're the Army and proudly proclaim

Verse:
> First to fight for the right,
> And to build the Nation's might,
> And The Army Goes Rolling Along
> Proud of all we have done,
> Fighting till the battle's won,
> And the Army Goes Rolling Along.

Refrain:

Then it's Hi! Hi! Hey!
The Army's on its way.
Count off the <u>cadence</u> loud and strong*
For where e'er we go,
You will always know
That The Army Goes Rolling Along.
* *"Two! Three!" is typically sung here*
but is not an official part of the song

Verse:

<u>Valley Forge</u>, <u>Custer's</u> ranks,
<u>San Juan Hill</u> and <u>Patton's tanks</u>,
And the Army went rolling along
<u>Minute men</u>, from <u>the start</u>,
Always fighting from the heart,
And the Army keeps rolling along.
(*Refrain*)

Verse:

Men in rags, men who froze,
Still that Army met its foes,
And the Army went rolling along.
Faith in God, then we're right,
And we'll fight with all our might,
As the Army keeps rolling along.
(*Refrain*)

[<u>edit</u>] U.S. Field Artillery (1917) [4]

(by Sousa, copyright and published by Carl Fischer)

Stephen A. Peterson

Verse:

Over hill, over dale
We have hit the dusty trail,
And the Caissons go rolling along.
In and out, hear them shout,
Counter march and right about,
And the Caissons go rolling along.

Refrain:

For it's hi! hi! hee!
In the field artillery,
Shout out your numbers loud and
strong,
And where e'er you go,
You will always know
That the Caissons go rolling along.

Verse:

In the storm, in the night,
Action left or action right
See those Caissons go rolling along
Limber front, limber rear,
Prepare to mount your cannoneer
And those Caissons go rolling along.
(*Refrain*)

Verse:

Was it high, was it low,
Where the hell did that one go?
As those Caissons go rolling along
Was it left, was it right,
Now we won't get home tonight
And those Caissons go rolling along.
(*Refrain*)

A Soldier's Prayer

Good morning Lord! How are You doin'?
I've never spoken to you before
And this prayer thing is new to me.
You see, Lord, my family and friends have always
Told me that you don't exist.
Like a fool I believed their foolishness.

Last night while in my foxhole, I looked up
And saw a cross made of heavenly bodies.
Right then and there I realized I'd been lied to.
If I'd just taken a little time to just look around
I'd see that living things
Are in order as are the heaven.
That can't have happened by accident.

Lord, I wonder if You can ever forgive me for
being so dad burn stupid!
Somehow I feel you'd understand 'cause
I believe you're bigger than my ignorance.
Funny, Lord, that I had to come to my awareness of You
In the belly of a foxhole.
Before I had time to know who You really are.

Lord, as I said before, I really don't know how to pray
But I'm sure glad I met You before it's too late.
I'm really happy I'm having this talk with You

Before I have to go off to war somewhere.

Lord, I've never been in a real war.
But I feel that this moment is the most
important day of my life.
If I should have to go off to war to defend my
nation's freedom,
Let me do so knowing You and having a
relationship with You first.
I don't fear for myself any longer for I now
know You.
I realize that You will be by my side.

Though I wasn't too friendly towards You,
I wonder if You'd be there for more of my
training.
Thank You for being with me here in this
foxhole.
Funny, since I met You this day, I don't fear
having to defend my nation.
Thanks Lord—good-bye! Amen.

(Said by an American soldier before he died in
Vietnam. Modified by the author.)

How Do You Say Good-Bye?

How do you say goodbye to your child?

Carl, the son of Dimitri and Sarah Dobinsky, was a joy to his parents, relatives and friends for nineteen years. He was said to be a happy, cheerful baby whose smile would light up the room. On his first day of kindergarten, Carl stood up for a boy he didn't know who was being bullied. When asked by the Principal why he did it, Carl responded: "Because it was the right thing to do! Isn't Josh a person too with rights? Just because he can't talk like me or you, why should somebody pick on him like that?"

Eleven years later as a high school sophomore, Carl pulled a family of three out of an overturned car on a lonely Oklahoma rural highway. Then he applied first aid to the injured father. According to the physician who performed the operation: "If Carl didn't take the action he did, the father would have died leaving a wife and a daughter to grieve their loss." When the family came to thank Carl for his bravery, he responded: "Ain't nothin' It was the right thing to do."

Finally, on May 8, 2001, with much anticipation for the future, Carl graduated from high school. Now it was on to college—to Oklahoma State University to study hard to someday become a pediatric dentist. Why? So he could watch the smiles of children when they came to his office needing dental care.

That all changed when on September 11, 2001, he watched from his dormitory television in horror the slamming of two planes into the Twin Towers in New York City. Following his classes, Carl went to his dormitory room to pray and think about the events of this day. Three days following the attacks on the Twin Towers, Carl decided to enter military service. On that weekend, he went home to discuss his decision with his parents.

"Why?" asked his mother with tears in her eyes.

"Mom, I've prayed about this. After I did, I've decided it's the right thing to do. Everything's gonna be okay, mom? You'll see!"

At the end of the semester, Carl was off to Basic Training to become a Medical Assistant in the United States Army. During training, a fellow soldier broke her ankle while negotiating an obstacle. Carl without hesitation or a word quickly took charge, stopped the bleeding, calmed the soldier, and splint the broken bone saving the soldier's foot and her military career. As he stood before the formation to receive recognition from the post commander, the General asked: "Private Dobinsky, what motivated you to help this soldier?"

"Sir, it was the right thing to do. I was there. I knew what to do so I did it," responded Carl.

"Bless you, Private Dobinsky! You're an outstanding soldier and a credit to the United States Army," responded the General tearfully.

Basic Training came to an end quickly for Carl and his fellow soldiers. Upon their graduation, Carl was elected by his peers and drill sergeants as the soldier of the training cycle for his hard work, dedication and selfless service to his fellow soldiers and to the United States Army. Called out from the formation, Carl was ordered to stand with the General in the review stand as the cheering Brigade passed in review.

One month after graduation, Carl and his unit found themselves in Iraq serving fellow service personnel and Iraqi citizens. While in Iraq, Iraqi men, women and children declared to the American command that Carl was a kind and gentle person who had their best interest at heart and that when they came for medical service or assistance, Carl was who they wanted to serve them. For to the Iraqis Carl became synonymous with the generosity of the American military personnel. Carl's name quickly spread far and wide in this ancient land resulting in families traveling for miles to receive service at the American medical aid station.

Then it happened. While on a mission to transport a pregnant woman and her husband to an Army medical aid station, a roadside bomb exploded disabling the transport vehicle setting it on fire. At that instance, Carl pulled the Iraqi woman, her husband and the doctor from the vehicle saving their lives though injured himself. He took up a defensive position to protect everyone from enemy fire knowing full well that he could be killed. When help did arrive, a shot ripped through the heat of the Iraqi summer striking Carl in the head instantly ending his life. Immediately dropping his weapon, a young 16 year old terrorist from Syria surrendered and was taken into custody by the rescue team of Americans.

When Americans and Iraqis learned of Carl's death, the outpouring of grief and loss quickly spread throughout the compound and surrounding area. As the sun rose on the following day, thousands of grieving Iraqis swelled outside the compound with wails and cries of death, the beating of breasts and the firing of guns into the air. At that moment, the cry of a little voice could be heard from the nearby hospital tent. It was a boy! To honor Specialist Dobinsky, the Iraqi couple named their newborn son "Carl".

Back in the United States, Carl was brought home. At his funeral, Carl's Commanding Officer was requested by the family to offer the eulogy. "How do you say goodbye to such a son and soldier? You don't. You weep and you let God share your tears. And you thank Him for the love, peace and joy that came into your life through him. For you know now that that part of your son, your friend will be with you forever! Whenever Carl did anything, he would always be heard to say 'it was the right thing to do'. To make the ultimate sacrifice as Carl did is the hardest thing he or anyone could do. To die for your friends and country as he did. May he rest in peace and love with his Lord, Our Lord!" as the officer tearfully took his seat with the rest of the mourners that day.

And may you be blessed as well. For in the eyes of God, it was the right thing to do. As the Father did many years ago that salvation, peace and unconditional love may be known in and by the world.

Onward Christian Soldiers!

My uncle Robert, a soldier who served with General George Patton in World War II, before he died told me of a battle for one of many key positions as Patton moved through France. American soldiers were reportedly trying to re-take positions lost to the German offensive commonly referred to as the Battle of the Bulge and were unsuccessful. Soldiers after soldier toppled, the troops began to panic. Up rode General Patton in his jeep to urge his men on. Encouraged by his presence, tenacity and bravery in exposing himself to the whizzing of German small arm fire, the troops began to cheer General Patton's presence.

"Don't cheer for me, men!" Patton called out to them, "Fight! Darn it! Fight! You're the better soldiers!"

As Christians we need to cheer our Commander, but we also need to get in on the fight. We Christians have Jesus Christ as our Commander, as King and in total control of everything. No one can defeat His Christian army and His Sacred Word. Jesus has stated that no one can take right and truth from those who are His Followers. We (Christians) are the better soldiers! There are people who need us! Darn it! Fight!
Now is the time to fight for our faith, for truth, for Christ—THE Commander-In-Chief!

Prayer: Almighty Father, it is so easy to talk, to be a bystander, so easy to sing Your praises. Now, Father, help me with the hard part.

Thought of the Day: Fight Christian soldier for your Christian principles and truth!

An Angel In Uniform

On a cold night in Kurdish Iraq, two young soldiers tried in vain to set up their squad's large tent as ordered by their Platoon Sergeant. Their problem was they brought their own wooden pegs instead of the reddish-orange metal ones.

"Mack," Danny said, "its going to be a real long, cold night if we aren't able to get this darn tent up." Mack nodded in complete agreement. In spite of having broken three wooden pegs, the two soldiers struggled on only to break two additional wooden pegs.

Then a Corporal appeared over the two soldiers' soldiers' shoulders, "You soldiers look like you could use a little, eh!"

The Corporal was about 6'5" tall and dressed in the same new Army Combat Uniform (ACU) as Mack and Danny. He, however, had a small sledge hammer and ten brand new shiny silver looking metal pegs. It took him no more than fifteen minutes with the help of Mack and Danny to set up the squad tent. Amazed at the speed the Corporal put up their tent, they stammered to thank him as the tall soldier moved on to help other struggling members of the Platoon with their tents.

"I was praying for somebody to help us." Mack muttered, "but I never expected an angel in a uniform."

Mack thought about the incident many times since. After careful consideration, he believed the

Corporal was an angel. Mack and Danny never saw again nor was anyone in the Platoon ever able to account for the big soldier's presence that early evening in Iraq. Several months after Mack's and Danny's experience, a near similar situation presented itself when a couple of struggling soldiers attempted to raise their tents in an Iraqi clay pan. It seemed as though it was a small pay back for a good deed show him when he was in need and desperate.

Why is this story being told? Well, just in the event you are skeptical regarding the existence of angels, you might be reminded to be on the look out. You might have been helped by one. Then too, you may very well be called upon the Master to serve as one!!!

Casting Stones Anyone?

While eating his lunch in any Army dining facility in Iraq, Army Staff Sergeant Alan Fischer met his long time friend Sergeant Robert Lopez. Staff Sergeant Fischer asked Sergeant Lopez how it could be that in the eleven years he had known him he had never heard him say an unkind work about anyone.. Sergeant Lopez just smiled as he swallowed the big bite he took out of his Philly steak sandwich. He reached into his left shirt pocket, pulled out a dollar coin size, flat, smooth gray pebble with a single word "First" written in back ink across it face.

"My grandfather gave this pebble to me years ago when I was a little boy," he explained. "Whenever I changed clothes, reach for my wallet or grab a pen, this pebble is someplace on my person to remind me that I'm not yet qualified to throw it at anybody." Finishing his lunch, Sergeant Lopez picked up his tray and disappeared among the growing crowd of service men and women entering the dining facility.

Later that evening, Staff Sergeant Fischer kicked over a small, flat, grayish pebble. He glanced at it at first then picked it up and put it in his pocket. When he arrived at his supply room, he took a felt tip pen wrote "First" on it then put it back in his left pocket where his wallet was. Now, when he sees that pebble, he reminded that an evil, unkind word or remark can hurt a person in the same manner as a five or ten pound stone when thrown in illicit judgment—all the more reason for not throwing it at anyone.

Forgiving Yourself...Is It Possible?

Sergeant Helen Meeks was wrong...and she knew it. It had occurred in an emotionally charge moment and now she regretted having said what she had said to one of her best friends.

"Amanda," Sergeant Meeks said, "I'm so sorry I flew off the handle when the C.O. was inventorying my supply area. I was wrong and I knew then and I know it now. Can you forgive me?"

"Alright," Sergeant Amanda Hull said. "Forget it. I'm good. I understand."

But Sergeant Meeks just couldn't forget it. She could not believe Sergeant Hull had forgotten it either. So when Sergeant Hull went to the Battalion Dining facility to eat that evening Sergeant Meeks once again apologized. Just before the two turned in for the day, Sergeant Meeks apologized to Sergeant Hull again.

That is when Sergeant Hull pulled her aside. "You don't have to keep apologizing, Helen. Really, I've forgiven you. I understand the position you're in. I also know that the C. O. can be one very tough cookie when it comes to inventories. But I really don't think you're forgiven yourself."

When Sergeant Meeks went back to her office, she thought about what Sergeant Hull had said. "I guess I hadn't! It all seemed too easy getting rid of a wrong so quickly and so painlessly. So I made myself feel guilty when

Amanda didn't seem upset and angry. And to satisfy myself I just kept on apologizing. But it didn't work. I was still paying when Amanda put an end to my charade and made me really look at the true meaning of forgiveness."

A few years have gone by since the day of her confrontation with Sergeant Hull. However, every so often Sergeant Meeks still has to convince herself that she is worthy of forgiveness even though it is written in the Bible that God has promised humankind forgiveness whenever he is sought: "Man, your sins are forgiven you" (Luke 5:20).

And despite what anyone believes, it is true! It is real! It is also that simple if one humbles themselves and ask for forgiveness of the Lord!

Lieutenant Sunshine

No one knew exactly who this bearer of good works was. She always came quietly and without fanfare wearing through the trauma and pediatric sections of the makeshift field Army hospital located southwest of Baghdad, Iraq. Because she wanted to remain anonymous she removed her name tag as worked her way through the complex. The only identifier she presented was her rank—that of Second Lieutenant. Yet when she left, there was a path of happiness and good cheer wherever she had walked. For her good work injured service men and women as well as hospitalized Iraqi children named her "Lieutenant Sunshine".

On Easter eve (Easter Vigil) 2006…she came at night carrying a large Army Combat color bag in her left hand. She slipped in and out of every dimly lit wing as quiet as a tiger on the prow and as quickly as she had appeared.

Later, when Lieutenant Julie Walsh walked down the narrow hallway to make her nursing rounds, she noticed small handmade baskets with a single chocolate egg on the table next to each patient whether that person was female or male. On the pediatric wing where Iraqi children slept were soft, cuddly stuffed dolls for the girls and small animals native to Iraq for the boys. Nothing fancy seemingly made out of materials possibly gathered from someone's extra items. A path of sunshine, happiness and joy to celebrate the day of new beginnings for humankind and a struggle nation/people yearning to be free!

Not a single patient in the hospital would ever know the name of the American servicewoman who brought the basket or the huggable companion to share her or his pains or separation from the ones they loved. She seemed to want no praise, no personal gratitude. Just the spread of the unconditional love of the Master of Love on His most triumphant Day! That seemed enough for Lieutenant Sunshine whoever she was!

A Bud Of Faith

For twenty-two days everything had been going wrong for Lieutenant Le Roi Brown. So much so that Lieutenant Brown's faith was slipping away as though pulled by one of the Army's heavy tracked vehicles. On a cold morning in Baghdad, Iraq as he and his platoon prepared to venture out to patrol the streets of the capital city, he prayed, "God, You seem so remote and aloof. Please give me a sign or something to build my weak and shattered faith this day. Lord, would you also protect me and my platoon from harm as well. Thanks, Lord. Amen."

As he combat unit slowly made its way through the hostile area, the voice of a crying child pierced through the early morning light. Focused on the sound, Lieutenant Brown and his soldiers moved quickly to secure the building. As each soldier moved into the house, Lieutenant Brown came face to face with a young woman huddled in a corner carrying an infant in one arm and holding the hand of an equally small daughter next to her.

"Come forward!" he said in Arabic. "We will not harm you.'

"All clear!" shouted Specialist Garcia from the stairs from an upper floor of the house.

"Ma'am, please come forward. You and your children will not be hurt. We will take care of you and them."

Without a word, the woman rose up with two crying children. She walked forward not knowing if she would live or die. She recalled stories that told of American soldiers brutally and cruelly stabbing Iraqi women then throwing their children against stone walls until they died of their abuse.

Shaking the woman said, "Do whatever you wish with me but please do not harm my children. My husband was killed at the police station looking for work three days ago so my children no longer have their father. My brother is in the next building with his family. He is hurt bad. He is not expected to live. He can't be moved. If so, he will probably die. He can't speak or communicate in any way. I've been praying that God would come to help save my brother, me and my children."

As she had stated, Lieutenant Brown found the young woman's brother and his family in a house to the south of the building he and his soldiers had occupied. Carefully searching the house, the man and his family, Lieutenant Brown and his unit quickly but carefully took the injured man and the two families back to their base camp where each member received food, clothing and the medical attention they needed.

After two days in the hospital, Lieutenant Brown visited the young woman and her brother. Very slowly and with difficulty, Lieutenant Brown spoke to the young woman who sat in a chair next to her injured brother. By this time, her brother though heavily bandaged about his torso could speak.

"Thank you, American." The man said, "May God be with you."

Lieutenant Brown's faith soared. For he knew he had been healed in his faith in God through this man and his family. In a few months, he was dismissed, alive and healthy.

As a thank you gesture to Lieutenant Brown and his unit, the once dying man and frightened sister gave him a tiny flower bud. A kind of an Iraqi flower that when given good soil and timely, generous amounts of water will produce a garden full of yellow and white plants of its species.

"Does this mean anything to you, Lieutenant?" the woman inquired.

"Yes," Lieutenant Brown replied. "This tiny bud you've given me represents a renewal of my faith in God and my friendship with you and your family. On the day I left to come into your area I asked God for a sign which I may build my weaken faith upon. God not only sent me His sign but he also send me you and your family. My miracle began with you, your frightened children and your dying brother to help build my faith in a hostile environment. God showed me that there are people who have more faith than I do even though they suffer beyond what I can even begin to understand or know. I can't thank you and your family enough for restoring my faith."

For this Caldean Christian, there was excitement in her voice to hear Lieutenant Brown's discourse as well as knowing that she and her family had restored a man's faith in the Almighty. She thanked God as well for the freedom brought to her country by a people she once feared.

Crossroads Of Life

While on the road to Baghdad, Iraq, the lead vehicle lead by Army Staff Sergeants Pete Sieford and Carol Blaylock had to make a decision. "The road map say we turn right at this crossroad," said Staff Sergeant Sieford.

"Right?" Staff Sergeant Blaylock responded. "It can't be. I thought we want to go north. If we turn right, we'll be heading south."

"Well, I don't know about that. I only know that the directions on this map say to turn right and not left, Sergeant Blaylock."

Staff Sergeant Sieford took out his map and compass oriented his map then shot an azimuth. "Yes, everything, the map and compass indicate we need to turn right at this crossroad to go north and to get to Baghdad. If we turn left, we'll head for the southern desert where there is just a lot of sand, no water, and nobody to provide us with any food either. Do you want to check it Sergeant Blaylock?"

"Well, no. Because I really don't know how to read a map or take compass readings. When I was in Basic Training I didn't pay attention to map reading or navigation along land terrain. I never thought I'd have to use them. But I feel that turning left will get us to Baghdad and not right. I just don't trust maps and compasses anyway. They're not always right anyhow. C'mon let's go left instead of right."

Staff Sergeants Sieford and Blaylock have a decision to make. Will they trust the mapmaker, their instrument of direction, Staff Sergeant's Sieford's use of these instruments or Staff Sergeant Blaylock? Will they trust the blind intuitions of a soldier who, by her own admission, failed to seriously learn the training she received during her time in Basic Training?

Sadly, so many people and soldiers in the Christian Army take the Mapmaker (God) and His compass (the Bible) as unreliable accepting, instead, the voices of unreliable even persons resistant to or hate God Himself. Some even have heard the Word of God and know about the Bible, however, by choice, ignore what they have been taught thinking it to be worthless. Rather than use the instruments given them they are satisfied with going blindly down the road of life using their intuition (human reasoning, risk taking skills, compulsive behaviors) then wonder why life is so difficult.

When the Improvised Explosive Devices (IEDs) of failed relationships, life threatening sexually transmitted diseases and death face these erroneous decisions, then we question the presence and very existence of God. In moments of grief and sorrow, humankind almost demand answers from God. When the response does not please humankind, God is blamed for being faceless, without compassion and mean spirited.

Instead, humankind must trust in the Mapmaker who stands with us at each crossroad of our lives, pointing us in the right direction. Today we know that this kind of trust is, very simply, faith—the assurance of things hoped for, the evidence of things not seen!

Folly In The Workplace

Colonel Stephen Weber looked out the window and saw a red Honda parked in front of his headquarters building. It had circled around the block for a fourth time making the Colonel suspicious. On the fifth drive around, the car parked then a driver who appeared to be an Army officer, sat still seeming to collect his thoughts. So at that moment, Colonel Weber decided to go out and see if he needed help. Perhaps he was lost and needed directions to a specific location. After all, this is a very large Army post and being new on post could be a very trying experience.

There was sadness in his voice. "I just wanted to get a good look at this building before I leave this facility. I will be retiring from the Army in roughly 30 days. I wasn't promoted so since I was passed over for the third time I am forced to retire as you know Colonel. I am Colonel David Ford."

Colonel Weber invited Colonel Ford in and as they walked around the office building, Colonel Ford talked about his plans if he would have been selected Regimental Commander. God is so good. It seemed like He saved this position for me."

Colonel Ford turned sharply and looked Colonel Weber right in the eye. "Well, Colonel Weber, that's great for you. Congratulation on your promotion to General, sir! It would seem you are a remarkable officer, but what does that say for how God feels about me, sir?" Then Colonel Ford told Colonel Weber the extent of his 30 year career in the United States Army that included three tours of duty in Vietnam, serious injury in battle, capture and escape from enemy soldiers attempting to kill him. Colonel Ford also told of commands in poor units and his ability to make them combat ready units in a matter of months. His willingness to sacrifice time with his loved ones in civilian and military schools for advance education was stellar. With tears in his eyes, Colonel Ford said his congratulations to Colonel Weber once again then left the building.

Colonel Weber replayed his exchange with Colonel Ford many times in his mind since then. He thought he was expressing his gratitude for God's expression of love to him in giving him his dream promotion to the rank of General—a position less than 99 in every 100 officers ever attain. But he realized later that what he conveyed to a fellow officer was arrogance and a presumption that God was exclusively on "his" side. In his own way and typical of too many of we who call ourselves Christian, the unwillingness to think through the implications of what we say to others, our neighbors.

Colonel Weber had no idea as to how his words impacted a fellow officer—perhaps God used them for good in his life in spite of him. But after prayers of forgiveness, Colonel Weber became aware of the need to submission to God's will; thankful for what he received in a quiet, non haughty manner; and listening to God's response. This episode did not stop Colonel

Weber from pronouncing the goodness of God to him and everyone around him, but he pledged his statements would be thoughtful, respectful and sensitive dialogue—not a glib, insensitive pronouncement unworthy of a Christian.

In God We Trust...Or Not?

After three days of what seemed like never ending tests, Sergeant Brett Mann was finally diagnosed, and now being wheeled into the operating room for surgery to remove his kidney stones. Even though Sergeant Mann had received a sedative to help him relax, he was very angry and agitated.

Though he tried his best to hide his anger, it showed because a nurse, Lieutenant Frances Santos came over, took his hand, and calmly said, "Good morning, Sergeant Mann, I'm Lieutenant Santos. You're a little nervous, aren't you?"

Sergeant Mann smiled weakly. "I'm more than a little nervous. I'm terrified. I've been through quite a few fights here in Iraq and that never scared me as much as this. I hate hospitals. They scare me to death! I don't know why. They just do," he told her.

Still clasping Sergeant Mann's hand, Lieutenant Santos said, "Well, Sergeant, just relax! There's no need to be nervous. Dr. Ellis is an outstanding surgeon. He is one of the best anywhere in the United States. In just a few minutes, he'll make you better than new."

"Well, I don't know," he said with a weak smile on his face.

Then Lieutenant Santos said, "You know Sergeant there are two ways to approach an operation. You can worry yourself half to death, or you can trust us. Like I said before, this surgical team here on the ground in Iraq is one of the best in the entire military or anywhere else in the United States. Really, you have nothing and I mean nothing to fear." Then she winked, gave Sergeant Mann a firm squeeze and said in a low tone of voice, "Especially since I'll be in the operating room with you making sure they do everything to standard. Nothing will get by me."

With those words, Sergeant Mann was finally able to relax.

Just as nurse Lieutenant Santos had said, everything went well. What Sergeant Mann remembered most about his entire hospital experience was nurse Santos' message. That is, he could approach life two ways—He could worry himself to death or he could trust. Though he accepted Jesus Christ as Savior, Sergeant Mann, much of his life before his surgery had a difficult time trusting—even Christ Himself. After a great deal thought and prayer, Sergeant Mann arrived at the conclusion that he needed to put his trust in God. "What's the point of calling myself a Christian if I don't or can't put my trust in Jesus who is God?"

What about you? In whom do you trust?

Meeting Challenges

At some point in every person's life, a challenge will arise that tests one's courage to do what is right. That said, there have been and always will be those who, through philosophical justification or fear, will fail to do what they can and should do.

Sergeant Major Curtis Braithwaite, a World War II, Korean War and Vietnam War veteran, was, in addition to a well decorated combat veteran and senior parachutist in the United States Army became a trainer late in his military career. As a trainer at the Fort Benning Airborne School, he was responsible for training many officers and non-commissioned officers to be fearless parachutist for the Army.

Some soldiers, now and in the past, became Airborne soldiers. But most, who reported for duty in the Army's Airborne School, did not earn this honor for one reason or another. Generally, the soldiers never conquered their fear of height or could learn to trust their equipment provided by the Army or their peers.

A young soldier, on his first day of Airborne School, came to Sergeant Major Braithwaite seeking individual lessons to become not only a parachutist but the best parachutist in the United States Army. The veteran soldier obliged starting the young soldier with the basics to overcoming his fear of height, then gradually increasing the height. Finally, the day came when Sergeant Major Braithwaite said to the young soldier: "Now, Private, the time has come for you to get up in the plane and jump out of a perfectly good plane. I've taught you everything I and the Army know. Come on, let's go with the rest of your classmates and perform! In my professional opinion, you're ready!"

Well, the young Private went up. But just before everyone was about to hook, he froze. "I'm afraid I can't do it, Sergeant Major!" he said in a low tone of voice then sat down as everyone lined up.

The Sergeant Major, in an unusual gesture, went over to the fearful Private put his hand on the soldier's shoulder. "Get up, Private! You can do it!" he said. "Look up to the bright blue sky. You'll see the face of God. He'll take your soul in His hand and guide you to solid ground and your body will follow you. If you can't trust me, your buddies and your equipment, then put your trust in Him. He will be your guide. He is your leader!"

A most unusual order? Perhaps. But the young Private understood the Sergeant Major. He moved to the front of the formation and without hesitation or another word said jumped into the Hands Of God.

Every Christian man, woman and child is a soldier for Jesus Christ. They always have been but fail to meet their leaders' call or prompting. Today, as it was in the past, Christians have been challenged to stand up and leap into their culture for Christ. Many are fearful as they have not placed their souls into the hands of their Captain trusting that He will take care of them wherever they may be or go. As the Sergeant Major said to the Private, "I have given you everything you need to succeed..." Jesus Christ has done the same in a hostile, resistant and openly bias society against Christianity. Now it is up to you/us to follow through without fear.

Sergeant Mike

Sergeant Mike, as everyone called him, had just undergone surgery to remove small pieces of metal lodged in his back and arms as a result of a roadside bomb. He was now alone in the recovery section of the Medical Aide Station Hospital (MASH) to think through what had recently happened to him. He and his squad of ten men were very fortunate while on patrol in a Baghdad neighborhood. No one was killed but two hurt. He being the more serious of the two. Sergeant Mike had faced and seen death before but it had always been the death of a fellow soldier—not his own, as military conflicts go.

At some point during his thought processes, Sergeant Mike realized that losing a fellow soldier's life seemed much more threatening to him than his own personal death. Lifting his inured arm above his head, he wondered why this was so. Then he remembered that each time he and his squad go out on a mission, he would ask himself: "Am I prepared to stand before Jesus Christ to receive His judgment?" His immediate response is: "Yes! Yes, I am. I am ready to meet the Lord without fear of His judgment."

With his readiness for death, Sergeant Mike believed he had nothing to fear during the course of his daily living. He felt he could live his life without fear or worry upon his physical death whenever or wherever that may be. As soldiers and military doctors passed Sergeant Mike's bed, he had the biggest smile on his face when a nurse came by to give him his breakfast.

An injured soldier in a nearby bed turned over to see Sergeant Mike. "Dang, man! Why are you lying there smiling? Didn't you come out of surgery just a while ago?"

"Hooah!" returned Sergeant Mike.

"Aren't you in pain and ticked off about your injuries?" responded the unknown soldier.

Then Sergeant Mike responded: "Not at all! I'm in the Hand of the Master! He promised that no one, not even death, can take me out of them. That makes me feel safe and secure. So why should I be ticked off? Yeah, I'm in some pain, but my pain is overshadowed by the sense of security I feel by Jesus being right here, right with now with me!"

"Man, you are freakin' crazy! I've never heard anybody talk like you," said the unknown soldier. But after a few minutes of thought. "Hey, Sarge! How do I get as happy as you and not be worried about stuff?"

"Just accept Jesus Christ as your Lord and Savior. He'll change your life. I mean it! You'll see! You will have a change in how you see life and living!"

"Really," said the unknown soldier.

"Yes, really!" returned Sergeant Mike.

Sergeant Mike and the unknown soldier prayed a simple prayer of acceptance of Jesus Christ as Lord and Savior. At the same moment they prayed, the unknown soldier felt a change he had never before felt.

"Wow," he said. "This feeling is a great. I feel as though a great burden has fallen from me. You're right. I really don't feel any fear of where I will spend my eternity when death comes. Thanks, Sarge! Why didn't somebody tell me about this before? As soon as I get better and outta here, I'm gonna talk to my buddies about Jesus Christ. Yeah, this is a great feeling!"

As the unknown soldier stated: "Why didn't somebody tell me?" There are many, many men and women out there who long for answers in their lives. You, as a Christian, have THE answers! It doesn't take much. Just a little happiness on your part and Jesus' assurances stated to others. So what are you waiting for?

When A Soldier Says Goodbye

One of the inconsistencies in Army Captain Amanda Rossi's otherwise devote Christian life was her disdain and fear of being separated from her husband and two children beyond 30 days. Because the Army needed combat engineers, Captain Rossi was ordered to active duty the initial days of the Iraq War.

Early in the afternoon of the second day of action, Captain Rossi's engineers received the order to construct a pontoon bridge across the Tigris River. Speeding into action, her engineers constructed a bridge in half the time the unit was expected. Within minutes of completing her mission, a single shot rang out hitting the Captain about the temporal region of the head. The impact knocked her 5' 2" frame to the ground. Stunned by the events, Captain Rossi's engineers rallied to medivac her still body to an Army hospital where she immediately went into surgery. When the 6 ½ hours surgery was completed, all the medical team and engineers could do was to wait for her motionless person to awake.

Four hours following the surgery, Captain Rossi's situation turned for the worst. She went into a coma. The doctors said unanimously that this was probably the end as she had lost so much blood and brain tissue. She came out of her coma, however, and her face was radiant.

"I saw Jesus, the Christ, the Messiah!!! I was back home again in a park in Oklahoma City next to Lake Overholser. A handsome man, who was actually satan, was there holding my hand. From a boat on the lake, Jesus could be heard from the boat to say, in a loud voice: 'Captain Rossi is my daughter, satan! You can't have her! Leave her this moment!' Satan covered his face then left. I was so happy."

For roughly a day Captain Rossi seemed to get better, then her pain increased—the most excruciating pain she had ever felt before and following her surgery.

As members of her unit came by to look in on their leader, one of the young Lieutenants, a non-Christian, verbalized his feelings: "Why couldn't Captain Rossi have died in a coma and be spared her pain. God is so cruel and evil! She talked about God. Why would God have her suffer this badly if He loves her? If that was me I'd cuss God out big time and tell Him where to go! I really don't understand any of this at all."

"Lieutenant," Captain Rossi said. "I'm not going to get better, I know that. But remember this moment and what I am about to tell you. In spite of what you may think there is God. Just because I am in pain does not mean He does not love me. He is preparing me for eternal happiness and He is telling me to tell you that He wants to be your Lord if you will let Him. Although you can't see Him, He is here looking at you and me with a smile. Remember this moment! Tell others what you have seen. Let them know I am so happy I cannot describe it!

When you tell others they will come to know the Lord as you will. Don't be sad! Be joyful! Go with happiness! Go back to Oklahoma, Lieutenant and tell my husband and children how much I love them. Tell them I have gone to my Father—their Father. Here, give them this cross I made while I was here in Iraq. Thank you, Lieutenant!

The next morning as the sun rose to bring forth a new day of life and hope in Iraq, Captain Rossi entered the boat with the One of her vision to sail to her glory. The young non-believing officer began to understand why she had not been allowed to cross her mortal life to eternal life in a coma. Jesus' concern had not been only for Captain Rossi's pain but for the Lieutenant's, all whom he will touch and you, the reader, as well. Had Captain Rossi died in her coma, the Lieutenant and many others would not have been reassured that she had seen and know the Lord was waiting for her and the Savior is real in a world dominated by doubt and unbelief. Nor would we know that she left this life with joy and much happiness!

Hopefully, you will be re-assured and your hearts and minds at peace!!

A Soldier's Tale

Master Sergeant Le Roi Brown carried a backpack that weighed more than 40 pounds. Despite the gentle rain of a South Texas summer evening, Master Sergeant Brown was hot—and the military unit he was attached had two miles to walk to complete this phase of their training during Operation Bald Eagle conducted at Camp Bullis during the summer of 2004. Suddenly, out of the waving heat looking like he had just stepped out of a Sir Conan Doyle Sherlock Holmes mystery novel, an American soldier dressed up in the traditional dress of an Iraqi stepped forward:

"American! Want to trade? Need food for baby"

"We must move on, sir," responded one of the soldiers.

"Need food for baby and wife. Like American food. Want to trade?"

"We'd like to but we must go," responded another soldier.

"Say, American. You don't look so good. You look worried about something," said the actor.

"No, things are fine," the soldier responded.

After roughly one mile had been completed, another soldier dressed in Iraqi dress showed up indicating he had information desired by the Americans. "Americans, I have good information. You want it? I show you. Okay! It not safe here. Bad people here! Hate Americans! Hate Freedom!"

Although the situation was for training, the assembled soldiers were shown a building housing people hostile to America's efforts. Shooting, though blanks, was based upon the situations experienced by soldiers who had been in Iraq and had returned. Following the training exercise, one of the soldiers acting as an Iraqi stated that while deployed to Iraq he prayed, "Lord, be with us as we work to liberate a people. May we see and recognize these people as our brothers and sisters whom you love. Lord help me to always accept Your help and protection in whatever form it comes."

Based upon a soldier's stories about his duty in Iraq, he wondered how often he and members of his unit met angels in the form and person of Iraqi men and women. Men and women seeking the freedom and liberties many Americans now take for granted. One thing Master Sergeant Brown realized whoever the Iraqis were, they were of God, sent to help him and the other men and women while they were in harms way liberating a people who lived through the horrors of repression, murder and death in their homeland.

Making The Best Of A Rough Day

"What a wasted day this has turned out to be," complained Army Sergeant First Class Sheila Barnes, Supply Sergeant, Company C, 1st Battalion. "Here I am exhausted, and I haven't accomplished an ever living thing for this day. The First Sergeant gave me this twenty-two page supply list and he expects me to have this list filled in five days! Help!"

Within two hours of receiving her "To Do List" from the First Sergeant, Second Lieutenant Ralph Cummings from the 2nd Platoon submitted a requisition for fifteen replacement protective masks and as many decontamination kits. He wants them within three days. First Lieutenant Miriam Meyers from 3rd Platoon submitted a request for twelve pistol belts, twelve canteens and twelve first aid kits. She wants them within a week as she wishes to send her unit out for a field training exercise (FTX). Sergeant Barnes' friend from a sister company, and a Supply Sergeant herself shows up full of worries about her runaway teenage daughter. She expects Sergeant Barnes to listen to and comfort her. And Sergeant Barnes' husband showed up for lunch at her unit filled with enthusiasm about having received his promotion to Sergeant Major. And their 15 year old daughter came home from school determined to tell her about everything that happened in school to include her "A" grade in advanced algebra and physics.

Within less than forty minutes the Battalion Chaplain, Major Brian Simpson and the Battalion's prayer group scheduled to meet at the Barnes' residence will arrive. Automatically Sergeant Barnes began to straighten up the coffee table, make some coffee; get the coffee cake; chase the dog out of the house; feed the bird; put away the dishes; pick up the Bible; it fell open to the Book of Job. She sees this verse. It's Job crying out: "Hear diligently my speech, and let this be your consolations." (Job 21:2)

Collapsing in the nearest easy chair, Sergeant Sheila Barnes thinks to herself, "A wasted day? Well, maybe I didn't accomplish one of the things I had been given or the things I wanted to. But all day I have listened. If just one person has been consoled, felt loved, felt important, felt needed, felt good about themselves by my listening, then I guess this day have been one of my better days!"

What Sergeant Barnes experienced is common to every working person at may stages or points in time in their work lives. They key is how we choose to seek relief in a busy stress filled day. Sergeant Barnes just so happened to access her Bible at a critical moment of her day. The Bible and momentary immediate prayer are always available to give one comfort and relief— and its free for the taking!

Suiting Up For Combat

Though only 19 years old, Jack Cain was considered by his fellow soldiers to be one of the most remarkable young men they had ever met. Private Cain was in the last few days of Basic Training when he received a call from the Red Cross that his father was killed by lightening on his way home from work. It was just one of three tragedies that visited Private Cain and his family over the past year. Just four months before this latest event, his family's house burnt to the ground resulting in the loss of everything of value. While the family was away attending Christmas services, house thieves broke in then destroyed or stole every present under their tree.

When Private Cain returned from his father's funeral, his senior drill sergeant marveled at how well he had survived his difficulties. Private Cain said, "I did it by putting on the whole armor of God."

The senior drill sergeant thought Private Cain was speaking symbolically, but he wasn't.

Then Private Cain explained how every morning before everyone else got up how he went through the motions of putting on God's armor, piece by piece, as outlined in Ephesians 6: 14-17.

"First, while lying on my bunk, I buckle on the belt of TRUTH, saying to myself—buckle of truth. Then I strap on the breast plate of

RIGHTEOUSNESS. Next, I reach over my bunk to get my shoes of PEACE for my feet. Then I pick up my shield of FAITH to protect me against evil. I reach over then snap on my helmet of SALVATION. Last but not least, I grasp my SWORD of the spirit. After these actions, now I believe I am ready to deal with the world.

"It may sound stupid and childish," he said boldly, "but I do not feel ready to be in the world until I am fully armored. I really believe when I do these things that God will protect me all day long no matter where I am or what I am doing. Every time I have not seen fit to armor myself against the devil, the world and the flesh unusual events and things have occurred to weaken me. I just don't feel right."

Outlandish! Absurd? Perhaps!

And then maybe not.

When Forgiveness Really Counts

Four months after returning home from Iraq, Army Specialist Brian Crow spent a great deal of his free time fixing up a 1956 Ford Mustang he called "The Tank". He tuned the engine until it could barely be heard above a whisper, and he polished the body as though it was a fine, ancient museum piece.

Within a week after he had put the final coat of polish on the car, it was sideswiped by a criminal attempting to outrun the police in a high speed chase. Luckily, Brian was not in the car, but it was judged a total wreck by two insurance adjusters.

Brian, however, did not think the car was a total wreck. As far as he was concerned, it was still a beautiful car that could easily be restored. So, instead of letting the car just sit in his driveway and rust away or attempt to sale it for junk, he decided to cut away the damaged parts, find parts in a junkyard and weld them onto the good parts.

Most of Brian's friends had their doubts about his decision to take on such a project. "Why spend all that money, time and effort restoring what was left of a car?" asked one of his Army buddies. "Why not just take the money the insurance company is ready to give your and buy another old car?"

Brian said, "When I get through welding the replacement parts to the damaged parts the car will be stronger than the parts that were built in the factory. A good weld is stronger than the metal it joins. Just wait you guys. You'll see what I'm talking about."

Will, Brian's friends did see. His car held up perfectly. What he told them turned out to be true. A good weld is stronger than the materials it joins. For one of Brian's friends, Sergeant Mack, "it's about having a good weld" has become his motto whenever he discusses toughness and the building of relationships to other members of his unit.

So whenever you have a disagreement or falling out with a family member or friend, think of this period as "welding time"—a time to rebuilt and forgive. Because forgiveness creates a stronger bond that nothing will be able to destroy!

A Little Christmas Story

Life in the State of Oklahoma is impressive all year but as Christmas nears no matter the size of the community, the 3 million plus residents of this plains state go all out to celebrate the birthday of Jesus Christ. Tulsa, the crown jewel of Oklahoma, has its shopping center windows blazing with brightly colored Christmas lights as children peer through their windows to catch a glimpse of the bearded old man in a red suit. While in Oklahoma City, Brick Town celebrates with a montage of beautifully praying angels surrounded by tall building. Lawton celebrates the birthday of Jesus with a living Nativity seen of unpaid volunteers. In each of these communities, though small by many people's standards, the joy, happiness and love for each other is rarely matched by any community.

Through Oklahoma's high hills and mountains, people make hast to find and discover gifts for loved ones and friends. Money does not appear to be a concern. The general consensus among many Oklahoman shoppers is money amounts are unimportant. It is the thought that counts. The gift or gifts say to the one about to receive it: "I love you," "I'm thinking about you," "You are special to me."

As Jesus' birthday neared in war torn Iraq, a small group of American soldiers from Oklahoma stationed in this ancient land, prepare for Christmas. A young Iraqi woman found her

Stephen A. Peterson

way to an America base camp in need of housing and food for her very young children. With her husband dead as a result of a suicide bomber and all known family members murdered or killed by Saddam Hussein, she had heard that Americans would help her in her plight. Desperate, she boldly demanded to see the American commander. She told her through an interpreter, she would be willing to work for food, housing and protection for her two children. Her name was Ahlam.

One task Ahlam was given was to keep an account of the food and clothing the American unit distributed to the local Iraqis. Ahlam kept a superb record of every thing distributed. At this time, however, Ahlam had a growing desire to thank the Americans who housed, fed and protected her and her children. At the time, having only work 5 days, Ahlam had very little money or means to purchase anything compared with the items she was recording and distributing each day. It seemed to her that the Americans from Oklahoma had every thing— lots of food, clothes and things. Things she had never seen or heard of were now before her eyes. These Christians women and men gave to any one—Islamics, Arabs, Kurds, Sunnis, friends or enemies.

Then, in the quiet and solitude of her American built home a few says before Christmas, a magnificent idea came to Ahlam. It was as if a divine voice spoke openly and clearly to her. The voice said: "My child, yes, you have suffered greatly. However, there are many who have suffered more. If you will pray and think about your concerns, you may find a solution to what concerns and troubles you."

Ahlam thought long and hard. Finally, on her day off, three days before Christmas, Ahlam was given permission to use the Post Exchange. Awed by the amount and volume of materials in the American store, Ahlam moved slowly along the crowded aisles mentally selecting the items she wanted then had them wrapped in brightly colored Christmas colors—red and green. Ahlam left the Post Exchange and faded into the cool of the Iraqi sunset. Since she had no male family members remaining to escort her outside of her compound, Ahlam received an escort from the Base Commander and two of her staff officers. Holding her package carefully and tightly, Ahlam walked into a Sunni area. Ahlam was a Kurd. Kurds were unwelcomed in Sunni areas. Ahlam's venture into this area of Baghdad was extremely dangerous, seemed foolish, impulsive, absurd for her and her American escorts. Then, through the roar of bombs and gunfire, she heard the cries of an infant. At once Ahlam felt better. During her dream, Ahlam remembered that the cry of an infant would be the indicator of who she was looking for.

Talking to a Sunni woman, Ahlam asked, "Can you help? I'm looking for an infant I heard crying in this area. I have a little present for the child."

The woman wrinkled her forehead, hesitating. Then with a smile she said, "It's almost two o'clock. We hurry to go to the markets to get what we need. We do this because it is dangerous to be on the streets when people go home from work. Foreign terrorist, bombers try to hurt and kill as many people as possible. But if you wait for a few minutes, I'll take you to the place of a child just born yesterday."

"Wonderful! Great!" said Ahlam.

Somewhere Special

It was 1320 hours when the helicopter landed carrying Army Specialist Jana Haney into a field hospital for emergency surgery. Thirty-five minutes earlier Specialist Haney was with her Combat Engineer Battalion setting up an electrical grid for the Iraqi city Najah when the unit was attacked by Islamist foreign fighters. In an attempt to rescue two Iraqi children from certain death, Specialist Haney was slowed when she placed the children behind barriers as Rocket Propelled Grenade exploded throwing her 5′, petite frame into the air. The children were spared. Specialist Haney, however, was seriously injured and now struggling for her life due to serious injuries to her head and a loss of a great deal of blood. Within minutes of her arrival, a team of the Army's best surgeon rushed to provide Specialist Haney the best chance of surviving.

After eleven hours of surgery, Specialist Haney lay in the post operative section of the field hospital to awaken. When nurse Emily Dutton checked on Specialist Haney, a serious problem with her vital sign arose. Nurse Dutton immediately called the doctors in who confirmed that Specialist Haney was in serious condition. Another surgery would have meant certain death as she was much too weak to try again. There was nothing more they could do for the twenty-two year old soldier but to watch and wait.

Early the next morning, the surgeon in attendance confirmed that Specialist Haney was in a coma. As she slipped away, her young soldier husband, who was also serving in Iraq, arrived to be by her side. He made no response to the suggestion that he leave the Specialist's side to visit with the chaplain or leave to get something to eat or rest. He seemed to be terribly quiet and deep in thought or prayer each time a doctor or nurse came by to check on his wife.

When his wife, Specialist Jana Haney was pronounced dead at 1420 hours, nurse Dutton was surprised to note that a white rose had been careful placed in her long blonde hair. Otherwise, the rest of the makeshift hospital room where she lay was bare and without anything except the young Specialist. Nurse Dutton ceremoniously let the young soldier husband out of the tent then watched him walk aimlessly into the scorching heat of an Iraqi afternoon to work through his grief. Then Nurse Dutton alerted his commanding officer and first sergeant of his wife's death and his general direction as the two children Specialist Haney rescued, a brother and sister, entered the tent filled with tears and grief.

On her morning rounds through the field hospital, Nurse Dutton noticed a small piece of paper protruding from a floral arrangement on a table near the area where the young Specialist had died. On the yellow sticky note were the following: "I'm sorry for having taken one of the hospital surgeon's white roses but when my loving wife and dedicated mother, Army Specialist Jana Martinez-Haney, went anywhere special she always wore a rose. It was her extra special flower. Thank you for your hard work and your understanding." Sergeant Brett Haney.

The Legend Robin Berg, United States Army

Robin Berg was the product of a biracial relationship. Her mother was African-American. Her father was Euro-American of Norwegian descent. When Robin was but three years old her mother was murdered while leaving the church on her way home. Believing himself unfit to take of little Robin as an over the road driver, her father abandoned her in a shopping mall in Oklahoma. Unable to tell authorities who her father was or where she was from, Robin was placed in state custody and put up for adoption.

For the next fifteen years Robin was moved from one foster home to another. When she reached her eighteenth birthday, she had been in thirty-one foster homes. Her first foster placement and most significant one was with an Air Force non-commissioned officer family of four. This Euro-American family wanted so much to adopt Robin but members of the African-American community fought such an adoption alleging her African-American. They argued that Robin should be adopted by an African-American family in order for her to maintain her cultural heritage. So this family sadly and tearfully returned Robin to the state after more than four years of loving care. During the four years plus, they taught Robin by their words and deeds about the unconditional love of God.

They taught Robin to put her trust in the Lord, to pray daily and to keep herself in her Bible. These things Robin did faithfully.

When the social worker came to take eight year old Robin away, the Air Force family shouted to her "REMEMBER, HIS PROMISE!" as they separated tearfully. Throughout her foster placements, Robin remained a devout Christian. Her faith never wavered despite cruel treatment, great sorrow, and often serious illness for overtly stating her belief in Jesus Christ as her Lord and Savior.

In her fourth foster placement, Robin was routinely mocked, deprived food and beaten for praying and demanding she be allowed to go to church to worship. Following a beating, her foster mother asked, "Robin, how can you know there is a Jesus and Heaven? Where is He? You are so stupid, ignorant and out of touch with reality! Come on girl! Tell me where this Jesus is! Why isn't He here to protect you?"

Exhausted from her mistreatment, Robin looked up with her hazel eyes shining, "Because I've got such a longing for my Lord right here," she replied softly as she placed her wounded hand over her heart. Robin's display of unrelenting courage and faith though being abused caused the foster mother to immediately order her out of her house as a child possessed by the evils of Christianity.

Finally, Robin became of age. She left her final foster placement with her Bible, two garbage bags of clothing, no money and no place to go. Though uncertain, she prayed, "Lord, I know You are with me. Show me what You will have me to do and where I am to go. I am in Your hands, O Lord!"

As she made a westward turn, Robin stood in front of an Armed Forces Recruiting Station. Something seemed to say "go inside Robin". Entering through the first door, Robin made a right turn then was greeted by an Army Recruiter. They both sat down to talk about a career in the Army. Robin was given a room in a local hotel to return the next day to begin testing and evaluation for service. Following her tests, Robin learned she was best suited for the position as a Chaplain's Assistant. She was certain the Lord was calling her to serve in this capacity. She joined the United States Army a week later.

During her Basic Training, trainers and peers were taken by Robin's compassion, dedication, loving heart and ability to endure difficult periods. When asked what was her secret in overcoming stress-filled moments, Robin replied, "I have a longing to do the will of My Father right here," as she placed her hand over her heart. "I am here for His purpose and His purpose only."

Within six weeks Basic Training ended for Robin and her peers. She went on to additional training as a Chaplain's Assistant. Following that training, she was sent to Iraq with Chaplain Michael Keith. Chaplain Keith was immediately impressed by Robin fervor and love for the Lord and willingness to go the mile to see to the completion of tasks he assigned her. Chaplain Keith could count on Robin to get the job done joyfully and without complaints.

On the morning of the celebration of the Resurrection of Jesus, two orphaned children, a boy and a girl, appeared at Chaplain Keith and Robin's compound very hungry and begging for food. Moved with compassion and love for these children, Robin invited them in and gave them enough food to satisfy their hunger and thirst before they slipped away into the Iraqi night. For the next six day, Robin's thoughts were on the two orphaned children and their whereabouts and safety. Then on the seventh day, the two children re-appeared. As before, they begged for food. Robin, once again, gave them food and something to drink. On this occasion, she inquired as to where they lived and their parents. Through the boy, Robin learned they were brother and sister whose parents had died as a result of a bombing two months earlier. There was no one they could turn to so they lived on the streets of Baghdad begging whenever they could. Their story broke Robin's heart as she recalled her own life story. Once again, the children left.

That evening Robin fell to her knees in prayer," Heavenly Father, I am worried sick about these two Iraqi children, your children. Show me, Father, what I am to do to help the boy and girl. Please, Almighty Father, I cannot bear to see and know these children live in harms way and could be hurt or, even worse killed. If they are killed, my heart will be broken. Please, Father!" as she shed painful tears.

The next morning Robin approached Chaplain Keith about her concerns for the two Iraqi children, "Chaplain Keith, I am worried sick about the welfare of two children, a boy and a girl, who came to our compound begging for food. I've prayed for guidance as to what I can do to help them. They have no parents. They were killed. They are living on the streets. I can't think of anything to do. What can I do Chaplain?"

"Robin, my daughter, you have a loving and kind heart. Continue to rely on the Lord. He will show you what to do. Just remember His Promise. Pray unceasingly for your answer. The Lord, in time, will answer you. Be vigilant and patient! I know this is not good enough for you but trust in Him. You'll see!" responded the Chaplain.

Robin knew the Chaplain was right but her desire to help the children weighed heavily on her heart and mind. In four days, the children returned. Robin fed them as she had done twice before. When they left, Robin followed them hoping to see for herself where they lived and how they survived. She hoped to try to convince them to come back to her compound to stay with her. Her plan was to convince Chaplain Keith and her commanders that she should keep the children, care for them and finally adopt them. As the children entered a white building, Robin followed as quietly as she could. When she entered, Robin found herself standing before Jesus Himself. Recognizing Him, Robin fell to her knees to give worship to Him. "Lord," she said. "It is so great that You are here with us!"

"Come with Me, Robin and enjoy forever the place My Father, Your Father, has prepared for you. You have been My faithful and loyal servant!"

Confused Robin asked, "What is going on? Where are the children, Lord?"

"They are here. They are my messengers sent especially for you. See they are right here!"

Standing before the Lord were the two children with smiles on their faces and praises of joy to God.

Robin asked a second time, "What's going on Lord? Where am I?"

"You are in heaven, Robin!"

"Heaven?"

"Yes! When you entered that building on earth, it exploded and you died instantly to enter your new life! Come and enjoy your new life forever in perfect happiness!"

The Saga Of "Big Tony"

Tony Pellegrino was a big man—6' 7" tall and 260 pounds of muscle.

They called him "Big Tony". He was big, all right, and loud and tough. Those who knew him swore he was the meanest man in the United States Army. A soldier in Big Tony's unit said he had the foulest tongue he had ever heard in his twenty-six of military service. And after finishing Ranger and Airborne Schools at Fort Benning, Big Tony went out drinking and rough—housing nearly sending another soldier to the promise land for making a comment he did not like about his mother. No, Big Tony didn't present a pretty picture at all.

Big Tony was sent to Iraq with strict orders from Division to follow the orders of his commanders and senior non-commissioned officers and not to get out of control. On his first patrolling mission, Big Tony was fighting angry when he warned the squad leader that he recognized an innocent looking device as a home-made bomb. It subsequently exploded injuring three members of the squad. While still in the field, Big Tony beat up his senior ranking sergeant causing him injuries enough to require hospitalization. Big Tony was given a company grade article 15 and article 32, 30 days confinement, a lost of a third of his pay and reduction in rank to Private E-3. Once Big

Tony got out of trouble, he was allowed to go on patrol. This time it was with a different unit.

During the patrol, the squad was engaged in a vicious fire fight. Big Tony watched in horror as a foreign fighter repeatedly ran an Iraqi through the heart with a bayonet as her children a boy and girl plead for her life. Their pleadings went unheard. When the foreign fighter grabbed the girl by the hair and was about to do the same to the young girl, that was all Big Tony could take. Big Tony leapt from his concealed position, ran towards the foreign fighter like a man possessed. With his rifle blazing, he killed the foreign fighter and three other comrades rescuing the sister and her younger brother. Members of Big Tony's unit stood stunned but cheered the Big Guy when he came back holding the hand of the young girl and carrying her brother on his big massive shoulders.

Like a guardian angel, Big Tony guarded the two children like they were his own daring anyone to adversely comment about them to his face. Taking the children back to base camp, Big Tony was surprised by the care and kindness members of the chaplain's team and other soldiers of the unit were toward these Iraqi children.

Big Tony knew about Christianity and, in fact, was a Roman Catholic. However, he rejected his Catholic faith when a young sister, whom he loved dearly died of cancer. He recalled praying long and daily for his younger sister believing God would heal her and make her better. When it did not happen, he angrily cursed God vowing never to trust God ever again. But when he looked into the eyes of the little Iraqi girl and boy he had rescued he witnessed the love of God. Big Tony could not believe his eyes and ears when the girl, a Caldean Christian, forgave the man and his associates who murdered her mother. The act of that 12 year old girl changed Big Tony's anger towards God suddenly and abruptly. With tears in his eyes, Big Tony went to the chaplain to tell him why he hated God. Big Tony asked the chaplain what he could do to make things right with God.

The chaplain simply smiled saying, "welcome back brother!"

Big Tony was stunned by the chaplain's response. The chaplain said, "Our God is big enough to deal with human anger and sin no matter how severe we think it is. Just ask for forgiveness. He'll forgive you and take you back. He loves you Big Tony. He doesn't care what you did in the past. This is now!"

When Big Tony came back to his unit that day he was a changed man. His habits of cussing, cursing, swearing, fighting and being a general nuisance were gone. His First Sergeant and Company Commander asked Big Tony what had happened to him. Big Tony told them in one quiet sentence: "I found the Lord Jesus Christ that was in me all along. I found him in this unit's Christian community and in the heart of an Iraqi girl."

Big Tony's story was a fact that has been observed over and over and over again down through the centuries since the Lord walked the earth in a human body: NO MATTER WHO YOU ARE OR WHAT YOU'VE DONE OR HOW LATE IT IS, THROUGH JESUS CHRIST YOU CAN CHANGE YOUR LIFE. Even if you are as vile as Big Tony WAS.

When Bombs Are Falling All Around

As a 21 year old Army Second Lieutenant Robbie Ducksworth remembered the day when a 16 year veteran Staff Sergeant came to the Lieutenant searching for a position in his Platoon. When Lieutenant Ducksworth asked the Staff Sergeant for his qualification, the Staff Sergeant boldly responded: "I can sleep soundly, Lieutenant, when the bombs are falling all around".

Lieutenant Ducksworth was not certain as to what the Staff Sergeant meant but he remembered what one of his West Point instructors had told him—"A wise NCO is your person as they are the backbone of your unit. Not you!" So Lieutenant Ducksworth hired the Staff Sergeant.

While preparing to go out on a mission in the roughest part of Baghdad, Iraq, Lieutenant Ducksworth ran around frantically checking on everything only to find all the armored equipment was handed out to every Platoon member, every soldier had the necessary ammunition and food they needed to accomplish the mission, and every soldier knew their responsibilities and could boldly state it when Lieutenant Ducksworth questioned them. All was well in the Platoon in spite of Lieutenant Ducksworth's fears and misgivings.

Then Lieutenant Ducksworth knew what the Staff Sergeant meant. The Staff Sergeant had done his job for him and the Platoon efficiently and faithfully did its assigned tasks without the Lieutenant having to worry. The Lieutenant had no need to worry when his Platoon faced whatever the enemy or the uncertainties of combat had to offer. The Staff Sergeant prepared the unit to meet any threat.

As a Christian, each person is in a battle for their faith every day! When a Christian hires Jesus Christ on as their top Sergeant, they will be able to face each day never having to worry about a thing! In order to accomplish this, three actions by Christ's soldiers are necessary:

1. Pray unceasingly. Too often many Christians believe pray is getting down on their knees. Okay, one may do so! However, one may pray walking to school, the office or to the park; taking a shower; while driving to work, laying in bed. A prayer does not have to be pretty or long. It may be as short as: "Thank you, Lord, for this water", "Thank you, Lord, for my comfortable shoes", "Thank you, Lord, for the two-minute rain" or ""The Lord is with me. The Lord is in me."

2. Commit to memory Scriptural verses and/or memorable song of praise. To do these activities is a simple method for making oneself aware of God's presence throughout the day. This also makes a person less of a sourpuss and to remember that a person is blessed in so many ways.

3. Do something to reflect God's unconditional love and presence to others. There are so many ways a person can reflect God and His unconditional love and presence. A few are:

a. tell someone God loves them
b. visit a sick person
c. talk to a hurting teenager
d. comfort a widow
e. give a little money to a hungry person down on their luck
f. comfort a mother or father who child has died
g. smile and be happy

These things can help one sleep soundly when the bombs are falling all around.

The Littlest Soldier

Fadi's mother's eyes were fixed on her seriously injured son as he lay in a United States Army field hospital room just outside of Baghdad, Iraq. Hospital personnel passing could see her heart was filled with sadness and anxiety. But they could also see she was determined to get help for her son injured by foreign terrorists along with some American soldiers. Like any parent, she wanted Fadi to grow up and fulfill his dreams. Now all of his and his mother's dreams appeared to be slipping away. Nonetheless, she wanted at least one of her son's dreams to come true.

She took Fadi's hand and asked, "Fadi, my son, have you ever thought about what you wanted to do or be when you become a man?"

"Mother, I've wanted to go to America, see the Statue of Liberty and some day become an American soldier ever since several American soldiers gave us food, a house and some clothes when father was killed. I want to know for myself where such kindness comes from mother," Fadi said through a smile.

Later that afternoon, she quietly walked over to the nurse's station where she met an Army nurse named Marilyn. She explained to nurse Marilyn that her son was seriously injured and asked if her son could become an honorary American soldier.

Nurse Marilyn responded, "Ma'am, I'm very sure I can get that done and more. I know about your son and what happened to him. I'll talk to the doctor about your son and send over a clothing specialist. I will have him make your son a United States Army uniform. Okay."

Nodding her head, Fadi's mother thanked nurse Marilyn then quickly returned to her son's hospital bed. As promised, a clothing specialist measured young Fadi. Four day later, Nurse Marilyn picked up Fadi's uniform and with a fellow nurse dressed Fadi in his brand new desert uniform with his name on one side and the U.S. Army on the other side. Once Fadi was dressed from head to toe in his new uniform, General Harold followed with 7 other soldiers to give Fadi a purple heart medal for his injuries, swore him in as an honorary soldier, and gave him a certificate making him an honorary citizen of the United States. Then two of the soldiers that were injured along with Fadi came to congratulate him for his bravery, becoming a soldier and an American. For it was the 8 year old Fadi who alerted the Americans patrolling the area that a strange car was near. When the car exploded Fadi took the brunt of the blast as the Improvised Explosive Device exploded injuring him seriously but causing minor injuries to the Americans.

That night the injuries Fadi sustained finally took his life. But before his dying breath, Fadi look up at the American soldiers, nurses and medical staff around his bed and asked, "Nurse Marilyn, am I really an American soldier and citizen?"

"I'll answer that," said the General. "You are an American soldier and citizen! Congratulations Fadi!" Everyone present cheered responding— "Fadi! Fadi! Fadi!

With those words, Fadi responded, "God Bless America!" He smiled and closed his eyes one last time. At dawn taps were played, a twenty-one gun salute rang out, a mother given a flag of the United States though her tears for her fallen little soldier.

When There Is Love

Outside the gate of a United States Army compound was a group of Iraqi citizens who looked like they were trying to gain entry. At the head of what appeared to be a small crowd was a young man beating on the gate. Immediately, a platoon size unit mobilized into action to defend against a possible attacked. When the officer in charge, Second Lieutenant Lars Petersen arrived at the gate, he discovered a man, his wife and relatives had a sick child with them. Lieutenant Petersen opened the gate then ordered the father, mother and infant be immediately transported to the Brigade hospital.

Within fifteen minutes of the family's arrival, the infant was found to be with an illness that no one on the medical team had been able to diagnose. Her temperature was 104 degree Fahrenheit. All efforts to bring her temperature down had been to no-avail.

As the man and his stood holding each other and in tears, Lieutenant Petersen lay down his M-16 rifle. With his Arabic translator approached the weeping parents. "Would you like to join us in a prayer for your daughter?" They looked then nodded a "Yes".

Lieutenant Petersen looked up and a nurse, Army Captain Agnes Chavez, and two other nurses came toward the small group. She had on a tray small loaves of bread and cups of a beverage for the weary couple. It seemed odd to Lieutenant Petersen at first that the group sat there eating bread and drinking a warm but the child's parents had been so stressed to think of food. It was obvious that they had not eaten in a while. When given the opportunity to eat a little was made available, they did so thankfully. Nurse Chavez ministered to the parents' spirits as well as to their bodies.

Then two of Lieutenant Petersen's soldiers joined the group to pray for the well-being of the Iraqi couple's daughter. After two hours of constant unending prayer, an Army physician came before the group to announce that the infant's temperature was subsiding, that she was out of danger and should recover without any brain damage. With that news, all the participants stood up, held hands and prayed... and cried.

Fifty-five hours of waiting and, praying resulted in the infant child's being able to leave the hospital as a well-baby. Before the man and his wife left, he stood up, raised his voice then said, "I thank Allah for my child's recovery. I thank you Americans for your goodness to my child and my family. All of my life I had heard Americans are evil and want nothing more than to kill Iraqis. I learned over the last few days that this is not true. I was surprised so many prayed for my child. I was even more surprised when you wept for my daughter. I asked myself 'why would do that?' I could believe what I witnessed. Thank you! Thank you! May Allah bless you all!"

Lieutenant Petersen and nurse Captain Chavez came to realize that there is always something one can do in a crisis. Even though seemingly small acts of love and kindness, they can be big as well as significant to someone else.

Redemption

Marine Private Mack "Buster" Kahle lay in Walter Reed Army Hospital, his body wracked with pain, on Christmas Eve, with little to celebrate for. Four months earlier, Private Kahle was out on night patrol when a small roadside device blew off a toe and badly injured the rest of his left leg cause breaks in eight places. The quick, efficient reaction of his fellow Marines evacuated him from the area of conflict and into surgery that made it possible save his leg. Following surgery, the main problem was the inconvenience of the cast. But as the weeks went by, Private Kahle began to experience intense pain. After being in a cast a little more than six months, the cast was removed and the source of Private Kahle was revealed. It was a problem he never suspected. Somehow the cast had caused the bottom of his foot to be worn to the point that the skin had not healed.

"How did this happen?" thought Private Kahle.

"Let's run some tests. I do, however, have suspicions as to what's going on," his primary physician said in an encouraging voice. "I just really want to be sure though. I don't like guessing about situations such as this."

Within two days, the results were back and not what Private Kahle or his physician wanted. Private Kahle had Type II Diabetes. Worse still was that the leg had to be amputated as gangrene had destroyed the tissue. Private Kahle was filled with rage and anger with findings and with his loss. Then his anger turned towards God.

"Why did God let this happen to me? I've always did what He wanted me to do! I go to church every week. I pray daily. I read a little bit of the Bible everyday and at times big parts of it. I give more than a tenth of whatever money and things I get. I help the poor, the sick and the troubled with my time, treasure and what talent I have. So why is God doing this to me? Why???"

As he lay in his hospital bed, he recalled that day he began his journey of faith as a Christian. His parents announced to him that they had decided to transfer him from public school to a private Catholic school. After a year, he decided to join the church. For him, that took care of his religious obligation. He prayed and was good to everybody around him. He came to learn, at least that is what he thought, every one else pretty much did. Private Kahle came to learn that God is to be feared if a person didn't do what God wanted them to do. So he worked hard at doing any and every thing he believed God wanted him to do. He felt secure that he was highly favored by God. Everything, for the most part, went well in his life as a youth. He could not understand why, of a sudden, things were going so bad.

"Private Kahle," a nurse said breaking his train of thought. "It's time. The doctor did arrive to explain the procedure, expected outcomes, and rehabilitation program he could expect to be in. It was at that moment he lost his fear of God. Mentally, he began cursing God. As he was being put under anesthetics, he hoped that he might not wake up. Maybe God might take him and relieve him of his perceived misery. He knew he wasn't the most religious person in the world and had sinned but he knew for sure that he didn't deserve what was about to happen to him. That was for certain. And he was going to let God know that too!

At 6:35 AM he reluctantly began counting backward was all he could remember. The next event he remembered muddled sounds of laughter and the words, "I think he's coming around. Good afternoon, Private Kahle. Call the doctor and tell him Private Kahle is awake," a nurse said calmly.

Now months of mental and physical pain brought Private Kahle on the road to recovery. He received word that a man and his wife thankful for his service to the nation donated funds enough to purchase a prosthetic leg. Within 21 months, he was able to do much of what he had done before his losses. Now back home again in Oklahoma he was considered a hero. He received a small town parade, married his childhood sweetheart and secured a good paying job. Everything seemed to be going great for Mack Kahle. In a couple of months, he and his wife were going to have their first child. Ultrasound revealed child would be a girl. Mack and his wife were elated. They began furnishing a side room as a nursery to receive their little bundle of joy.

As Mack began assembling the baby bed, he began to experience a deep sharp pain in his back. At first, he thought it was the affects of having wolfed down a larger than normal meal of lasagna with a dozen dashes of Louisiana hot sauce. When he dropped to the floor, an ambulance was called to have him transported to an Oklahoma City hospital 85 miles away. The medical team determined Mack Kahle needed a liver transplant as soon as possible even though his medical problems posed an enormous risk to his life. Mack's stress was increased when he was told following his medical evaluation that he would have to be approved of a transplant. He knew this was not a certainty because of his diabetes. And even if he was accepted for a transplant, he knew he would be placed on a waiting list. This could take months maybe even years. He also came to realize that if the transplant was made available to him, the operation may not result in success.

After ten days of waiting, Mack was accepted for the transplant list in spite of his diabetes. Though relieved, the waiting would be just as torturous. What could he do? He called God everything but "Holy". "How could God be compassionate to me after I cussed Him, cursed Him and disowned Him?" He knew, though, that God IS the One who could extend his life on earth. Quietly, and with little fanfare, Mack made his peace with God.

Thirteen months following placement on a waiting list, the doctor called to tell him that a liver had been found. Mack took the news as a blessing from God and as a sign that He had forgiven him his indiscretions toward Him. Then as his elation settled, he realized someone had or would die. The doctor entered Mack's room to inform him that a twenty-six year old woman, wife and mother of two will more than likely not survive beyond a day or two.

Mack spent the waking part of his day grieving over the thought that a young woman, wife and mother was dying that he may live. Also going through his mind was how the woman's family must feel after being asked for their sacrifice of a vital organ their loved one. He, at that moment, prayed for their solace and comfort in their most difficult time. He thought less about himself ashamed that he had been unfaithful to God because of his problems. Perhaps he would survive this surgery. If he did, he promised he'd thank God and the woman and her family for their sacrifice. God, in His own way, had made him grateful and thankful for all that he had.

Six months following his transplant, the doctor who performed the surgery informed Mack that his body had miraculously accepted his new liver and that his rapid recovery, from a physical standpoint, was a miracle. The doctor's report as well as the incidents leading to the moment made Mack realizes that indeed there is a compassionate, forgiving God who is bigger than any human indiscretion. When anyone asks, Mack tells them that God saved on the battlefield, gave him a new leg and a new liver to spread His Word, tell all there is nothing one can do wherein God will not forgive them and that they should prepare themselves for his eventual coming each and every day.

Marines

Marine Song

From the halls of Montezuma,
To the shores of Tripoli;
We fight our country's battles
In the air, on land, and sea;
First to fight for right and freedom
And to keep our honor clean;
We are proud to claim the title
Of United States Marine.
Our flag's unfurled to every breeze
From the dawn to setting sun;
We have fought in every clime and place
Where we could take a gun;
In the snow of far-off northern lands
And in sunny tropic scenes;
You will find us always on the job
The United States Marines.
Here's health to you and to our Corps
Which we are proud to serve;
In many a strife we've fought for life
And have never lost our nerve;
If the <u>Army</u> and the <u>Navy</u>
Ever look on Heaven's scenes;
They will find the streets are guarded
By United States Marines.

From Wikipedia, the free encyclopedia

Jump to: navigation, search

The "**Marines' Hymn**" is the official hymn of the United States Marine Corps. It is the oldest official song in the United States military.[1] The song has an obscure origin—the words date from the 19th century, but no one knows the author. The music is from the *Gendarmes' Duet* from the opera *Geneviève de Brabant* by Jacques Offenbach, which debuted in Paris in 1859. The Marine Corps secured a copyright on the song on August 19, 1919, but it is now in the public domain.

The initial verse is "From the Halls of Montezuma to the Shores of Tripoli." "Montezuma" refers to the Battle of Chapultepec, which took place during the Mexican-American War; "Tripoli" refers to the First Barbary War and the Battle of Derne.

The "Marines' Hymn" is typically sung at the position of "attention" as a gesture of respect. However, the third verse is also used as a "toast" during events important to the Corps such as the Marine Corps birthday, promotions, and retirements. Note the line "Here's health to you and to our Corps."

The Colonel

In the middle of his fifth deployment to Iraq, Marine Sergeant Tony Dunn was seriously injured when his lower left leg was blown away during a battle with insurgents. Many Marines, former high school classmates and friends called, wrote letters and sent e-mails to inform Sergeant Dunn that they were praying for him and for his speedy recovery from his injury. Sergeant Dunn stated and wrote a general appreciation statement that every call and every written form of communication was received with gratification for the many prayers and well wishes received from everyone who wished him well. One letter, however, stood out in particular. The letter was one he received from a retired Army Colonel.

The Colonel wrote: "This is the prayer I pray for you every morning at seven o'clock: Almighty God and Father, shine Your healing light on Sergeant Tony Dunn, lovingly heal his mind and his body of the pains of war and restore his spirits. I pray in the most Holy Name of Jesus Christ, Our Lord, that Sergeant Dunn will continue to believe in You, be restored to good health and live joyfully throughout the days of his life. These things I pray. Amen."

Seventeen days after Sergeant Dunn received the Colonel's letter, he was visited by him in Walter Reed Army Hospital. Like Sergeant Dunn, the Colonel had no legs and was confined to a wheelchair. His gray haired fatherly figure and wide smile touched Sergeant Dunn aiding in his recovery. The two men became instant friends.

By visiting him, telling him when he would be praying for him and what he would be praying for gave Sergeant Dunn something specific that he could hold on to. Also knowing that he had suffered very similar injuries help him immensely. For he knew the Colonel had gone down a similar path in life as he (Sergeant Dunn) had gone. Sergeant Dunn knew that every day the Colonel would he present in spirit, through prayer, even though he may not be so physically.

After his experience, Sergeant Dunn decided that when someone needed his prayers that he will remember that warm, glowing gesture of his new friend, **the Colonel**.

A Precious Gift

Marine 2nd Battalion 3rd Brigade 5th Marine Division had a blood donor program whereby if a Marine donated a pint of blood that individual could take a day off if being off did not conflict with Platoon or Company missions. Viewing this as an opportunity to get a little time off, Sergeant Norman Fritz decided to sign up. As Sergeant Fritz waited his turn, he began a conversation with Private Justina Collins, a young Marine who had only been out of basic training just 8 months ago. He asked Private Collins what she would do with her free day on a 100 degree day in Baghdad.

Private Collins indicated that she had no interest in having a day off. "That's not why I give my blood," the Private said boldly. "I give because I have received."

Private Collins went on to tell Sergeant Fritz how, while only being in Iraq for seven weeks, she was injured in a roadside bombing attack followed by small arms fire. After receiving major surgery to remove bullets from her hip and chest, she awoke in the recovery room so cold she thought it to be winter in Baghdad. Piles of military blankets did not help. After evaluating her situation, the medical team decided she needed a transfusion of whole blood. Though barely conscious, Private Collins reported she could feel the precious blood make its way through her starved arteries and veins.

She could actually feel every fiber of her being warming up and a renewal of life.

"It was the most beautiful feeling I have ever experienced," she said. "As I lay there in that hospital room, I thanked God, the doctors and my fellow Marines who cared enough to give me the blood I needed to live. I now give my blood that others may live."

At that moment Sergeant Fritz felt so ashamed. Sure, donating his blood would help perhaps another Marine, maybe other Service Members or maybe even an Iraqi citizen. But he knew he was not giving for the right reason. As a Christian, Sergeant Fritz knew, since he became of age, that Jesus Christ gave His blood unconditionally for him and every person for all time. Like, Private Collins who experienced the life saving blood of fellow Marines, Sergeant Fritz felt a renewed salvation and warmth of the Blood shed by the Son of God on his behalf. Sergeant Fritz realized more fully the mystery of His death because He cared enough to sacrifice every drop of His blood for him. At that moment, Sergeant Fritz could feel a warming of his being and a renewal of his spirit like he never, ever experienced before. Sergeant Fritz apologized to the Lord for his moment of selfishness with a self reflective, rhetorical question: "Will I ever really learn to care as much for others as Jesus did for me and all of humankind? Probably not—but I can begin to try this very day.

What about you?

Starved? Thirsty?

To avoid capture by a group of foreign fighters who had filtered their way into Iraq, Marine Corporal Nadia Murphy roamed seemingly without direction in the Iraqi countryside to avoid capture. For fifty-three days, Corporal Murphy survived until she was spotted and received by a helicopter of the United States military out searching to find her.

"I was so hungry," she told the Navy psychologist, "that I ate whatever live insects I could get my hands on, consumed grass, and drank muddy water I strained through a handkerchief to satisfy my thirst". Only her strong faith, she admitted, kept the young Marine from losing hope that she could survive to be found in a combat situation.

Few people in the industrialized world know what it is like to go without food or something to drink for long periods of time. Those who are told of a person having to eat something repulsive to them or described being so hungry and thirsty that they would be reduced to such action is an unimagined bad dream. A bad dream wherein one might hear a person say, "I would never, ever do such things no matter how bad off the situation was".

Similarly, there are so many biologically living people (often referred to as the "walking dead") walking about with unfulfilled spiritual hunger and thirst—a deficiency that for some last a lifetime however long. Some bounce from one religious or intellectual experience to another without any degree of satisfaction to speak of. They easily fall into addictive lifestyles (food, substances, sexual promiscuity, things) where the profane become sacred. Why? Some people are without light, without awareness that a relationship with God will satisfy their longings. Others have intellectually rejected God as a source of help due to spiritual blindness and outright human arrogance.

What does it take to change the attitude of these people? The answer in every situation is an intense need that often results from some traumatic experience or when the person is broken and, as it is said, "hits bottom' in their personal life. It is when he or she is helpless and in great need that Christ is most real. The greatest of Christian stories of ordinary men and women who attained their Christian faith have generally experienced such a need as Christ expressed in His beatitude: "Blessed are they who hunger and thirst for righteousness; for they will be filled". (Matthew 5:6).

If you feel spiritually hungry and/or thirsty or if someone known to you is so, note Christ's condition for being filled is a hunger and thirst for righteousness that is spiritual. In other words, a person must want Him intensely with her or his entire being—body, mind and soul to be filled or satisfied. A half-hearted attempt or a religious experience will result in unfulfillment and emotional confusion and loss.

The Little Iraqi Girl

Each afternoon at the end of his duty day, Marine Private Ernie Towe attempts to make it to the hospital to see a little Iraqi girl who was 9 or 10 years old. Private Towe and his squad found the girl in a building terrorists used to manufacture car bombs. On the day the little girl was injured, a bomb exploded killing everyone in the building except the little girl. When the Marines found her she was near death but led by Private Towe her battered body was brought to the field hospital where doctors immediately performed life saving surgery on her battered body. In addition to this sorrow, surgeon determined her to have Hodgkin's Disease. The surgical team wanted to begin treating her cancer but felt she was so weak that such treatments for the time being would surely kill her. So they put off the treatments for now.

One hot afternoon Private Towe walked from his living quarters to the hospital. As he walked towards the hospital, he noticed his footwear was especially unattractive. These combat boots had seen their better days in the sands of Iraq. "No point in putting on a new pair of boots at this moment. I don't think the hospital staff would care if I walked in these. After all I just came off duty. And the little Iraqi girl won't care either. She probably has to deal with her pain to give it much thought."

But then, in a flash of anger about the present situation and concern for the little girl, Private Towe returned to his quarters. Without a great deal of thought, he put on a brand new pair of military boots. But before he left he shaved and took a shower. He then set off for the hospital. Everything felt right then.

When Private Towe arrived, he realized he could not talk to the little girl without a translator. Finding a translator among the staff, he said a few words to the little girl whose name he did not know. He, at that point, was moved with emotion upon seeing the motionless figure of the little girl in a multiple layer of bandages. "Little girl," he said, "I will pray to my God that you get well, but more so that if you cannot get better He will take you to His heart where everyone is happy and where there is no more pain." At no time during the visit did she respond. He was not sure if she could even hear anyone. Running out of things to say but not wanting to just sit in silence, Private Towe said, "and little girl, I have on my best uniform and a brand new pair of boots I just bought. I wanted to look my very best to visit you and to pray for your well being." And as he said these words, the little girl's weakened arm lifted to touch the face of Private Towe then his hand. She squeezed his first two fingers seemingly as a gesture of thanks and appreciation for all that Private Towe had done for and on her behalf.

Not long after Private Towe's visit that day, God gave the little Iraqi girl rest from her suffering. That evening Private Towe received the news of her death and wept as he prayed once again that her soul would be with the Lord. But every time Private Towe put on that pair of boots, he remembered that afternoon when the little Iraqi girl, his special friend and child of God, showed her gesture of thanks by extending her injured hand to thank him for her rescue and to the wonders and joys of the Almighty.

You May Rest Assured

Marine Lance Corporal Tab Hansen, while on his very first combat mission in Iraq, was deeply frightened far beyond his comprehension despite all of the training and support he had received throughout his brief military career. Just ten minutes earlier his Platoon Leader, Lieutenant Courtney Holloway, was shot by a sniper's bullet meant for him if the Lieutenant did not shield the Lance Corporal. Having cleared the area, a steady stream of helicopters gathered in the area to remove dead and injured Marines. Marine companies were instructed to remain in the area pending order from higher headquarters—a fairly standard Marine procedure following combat action to secure the area.

Not understanding the situation, but sensing its gravity nonetheless, Lance Corporal Hansen huddled alone beneath the shade of a huge palm tree behind a house—until suddenly the quietness seemed overwhelming and he panicked. Crying out in utter terror, Lance Corporal Hansen got on his feet, picked up his M-16 weapon, then ran toward what appeared to be a Christian church. Entering its sanctuary, it seemed gloomy, dark and bleak. Immediately, he felt a warm, familiar hand over his shoulder followed by his re-assuring voice. His Company Commander, Roger Lighty, a veteran of more than a dozen combat missions who likewise sought the solace of the church. As was his habit following any mission, Captain Lighty took time to thank God for his life, health and fellow Marines. Captain Lighty's presence made Lance Corporal Hansen feel as though no matter what was going on in the battle zone, everything would be alright. For Captain Lighty was a man of outstanding leadership skills that Marines in his Company as well as the adjacent Companies and Battalion came to recognize and understand.

To this day, it was not the heat of combat, the injury to his Platoon Leader, or the sound of incoming helicopters Lance Corporal Hansen most recalled. It was the memory that his Company Commander, Captain Lighty was with him at a time of his deepest emotional and spiritual need. He heard the Lance Corporal's prayer as he followed him to the church and prayed with him. This gesture removed his fear for the moment.

Everyone, regardless of their condition, can have the same assurance from God. You who read this little story may be crying out for comfort and peace in your personal combat with hatred of another, lust, unjustified anger, greed, or an unwillingness to forgive another of their wrongdoing. Will what burdens you be immediately and completely eased? Not always! But the blessed assurance promised and granted by Jesus Christ Himself is His binding contract to humankind that He is with you. Therefore, you are never alone. Jesus Christ, your Brother, is always present anywhere you are...as you combat and struggle with evil and the evil one!

A Friend Indeed

There was a flash then a loud boom. It was as though Marine Sergeant Kirk Mac Murray was watching everything in slow motion. When the smoke cleared, Marine Private Lester Williams lay wounded from a roadside bomb blast. Within a matter of minutes, Marines emerged to see to Private Williams' wounds. In less than ten minutes, he was in an Army hospital.

Two young doctors examined the leg carefully. At first, the doctors considered amputation as their only alternative. What changed their original diagnosis were the pleas of Private Williams. He believed his leg could he saved in spite of his injuries.

One of the two doctors turned to Private Williams, "There's going to be a great deal of pain, but if you're wanting to try, let's work towards saving your leg."

Sergeant Mac Murray sat next to Private Williams, and prayed for the next six hours, while the surgeons carefully and as gently as they could labored to save his leg.

After three days, gangrene set in. In spite of anesthetics, the pain to the young Marine was excruciating, yet the doctor would not give up nor did Private Williams or Sergeant Mac Murray.

This event was in 2005. Private Williams has his leg to this day. He walks as though no such injury ever occurred. Thanks to God, a surgeon who refused to take the easy way out as well as a stubborn prayer warrior in Sergeant Mac Murray, Private Williams does very well today.

Private William's story is an illustration of a young man who demonstrated a great deal courage. Anything worth saving whether personal or even a nation is worth the pain. Jesus, Himself, did not take the easy way out, either. He suffered, excruciating pain to free humanity.

Being Careful Of What You Wish For

His name was Chris Jessup, a Lance Corporal in the United States Marine Corps. Many members of his unit considered Lance Corporal Jessup bossy, arrogant and thought he knew just about everything. Several squad members, including Private Fuqua, prayed for the day when they did not have to be around the Lance Corporal. Nonetheless, Private Fuqua and Lance Corporal Jessup almost always seemed to end up on the same details—examining Platoon waterlines; checking ammunition levels; calibrating the unit's caliber 50 machine guns to name a few unit activities.

Then Lance Corporal Jessup was transferred to another unit. At first, Private Fuqua was delighted. He was finally rid of the Lance Corporal. Then he noticed that activities in the Platoon were not functioning as smoothly as before. Had requisitions for field rations been ordered on time? No. Were the dozen or so night vision equipment inspected prior to going out on patrol? No one really knew how to do key Platoon activities as quickly as the Lance Corporal nor did they have any idea of what they were doing. Did anyone know how to speak Arabic like Lance Corporal Jessup? No. In fact no one knew any Arabic when Lance Corporal Jessup was transferred. Within two weeks after Lance Corporal Jessup's transfer, Private Fuqua began to appreciate the now departed Lance Corporal.

"You bet he was bossy," thought Private Fuqua. "But he was also well, organized, efficient and willing to go the extra mile to do the hardest, sometimes most challenging tasks."

At the end of the first month after Lance Corporal Jessup had gone Private Fuqua wished he had tried to know him a little better. Maybe the Lance Corporal would not have been the bossy, arrogant and difficult person he was thought to be.

Many of us actually search out and find the negatives about a person we do not like. Their flaws become larger than they actually are. Once they are gone then we come to realize that maybe that person was not so bad after all. What if the Lord did to us what we tend to do to each other at one time or another—even Christians to other Christians. What we perceive to be misgivings and faults, are useful, beneficial behaviors or acts that may help us through our earthly journey. But each time we meet someone who seems absolutely impossible, take a fresh look at that person and always find something wonderful and good.

From The Heart

During the summer of 2006, a young Iraqi girl and her father made their way to the American compound to see Marine Second Lieutenant Phoebe Watkins.

She was carrying some exquisite material as she walked just behind her father. They arrived at the Marine compound and were permitted to enter. Although neither she nor her father could speak English, Lieutenant Watkins could understand by their gestures that she wanted the Lieutenant to make her a beautiful wedding dress. This unusual situation between two cultures arose when Lieutenant Watkins helped another young Iraqi women design her wedding dress a little more than a month before. Lieutenant Watkins, a college graduate majoring in fashion design from Oklahoma State University, took this as a friendly gesture and to do her part to advance good will between the United States military and the Iraqi people took on these projects. She did so cheerfully.

After Lieutenant Watkins nodded her approval to the woman and her father, she began measuring her to begin the dress making process.

Within ten days the dress was finished, the young woman came to see Lieutenant Watkins for her final fitting. Her father's expression of approval needed no words. She was beautiful by any cultural measure. She turned from the mirror, gave Lieutenant Watkins a hug and went into a lengthy speech in Arabic. Her father, likewise, did the same.

Lieutenant Watkins heard the father and daughter out, nodding now and then though she didn't know any Arabic. When the young woman and her father had left, Lieutenant Watkins' Commanding Officer asked her, "Lieutenant, why did you let her and her father go on and on when you didn't understand a word they were saying?"

Lieutenant Watkins simply said, "You're right, sir. I don't know any Arabic. But when someone speaks from their heart, regardless of their language, I understand, sir. And by this and any other projects I may have, I hope I'm advancing my God, my country and good will among people. That's my hope and prayer, sir!"

Life Anyone?

Marine Captain Michael Lewis, a counseling psychologist, was making his rounds visiting with hospitalized military service members when he came upon Marine Sergeant Alvin Searcy. Sergeant Searcy had been sentenced to life in a wheelchair as a result of an Improvised Explosive Device (IED) while serving on military duty in Iraq. Though understandably devastated by his prognosis, the injured Marine had made excellent progress.

"Do you mean physically, Captain?" asked Sergeant Searcy's Battalion Commander, a veteran Lieutenant Colonel.

"No, mentally and spiritual, Colonel." The psychologist explained it in this manner: "My first question to Sergeant Searcy was 'Do you want to live or not?' Before his injury I was told that the Sergeant lived a very active life, and the thought of a sedentary existence left him uncertain about his future and life in general. I immediately let him know that if he didn't want to live anymore, I could no longer help him. If he did, we could explore his possibilities together." The paralyzed Marine, though still uncertain about a few things, decided he did, in fact, wanted to go on with his life. He was asked to prayerfully consider his tomorrow. He indicated in my most recent conversations with him, a desire to become a physicist."

Stephen A. Peterson

The Sergeant's Battalion Commander was surprised by the psychologist's blunt question about wanting to live, but when he considered the alternatives, he readily agreed with the therapist that it was a critical question.

Unless we say "yes" to life, and it is well-documented throughout the annals of history, the human spirit cannot triumph. Half hearted living is no living at all. It is comparable to one's faith. Lukewarm, tepid faith is really no faith at all. Fortunately, God has planted a strong desire to live and survive in each of us. Some call this the "survival instinct". That is, a force that resists death to the end. The mystery that remains and has been debated among some of the most brilliant minds down through the centuries continues to be why it so often takes a life threatening act or event for humanity to discover life's absolute preciousness and its true purpose and meaning.

A Special Little Visitor

Marine Privates Curtis Crownover, 20, and Antonio Palacios, 19, sat in their assigned position during the fighting for the Iraqi city, Fallujah preparing to eat their MRE (Meal Ready To Eat). Out of nowhere, a young Iraqi boy about seven or eight years old, homeless and hungry, appeared. Immediately, both Marines trained their rifles on the boy who, without fear, simply walked forward towards their position. Seeing that the boy posed no threat, the Marines lowered their weapons then signaled for the youngster to come in. When he sat down, his eyes instantly fixed on the Marines' food bags. Both knew the boy was very hungry.

"How about some Mexican rice?" said Private Palacios.

"We can share some of my chicken. Taste it! It's real good tasting chicken kid!" as Private Crownover handed about half of his ration to the boy.

Without hesitation, the boy began quickly stuffing food into his mouth chewing so quickly the Marines thought he might choke.

"Whoa!" responded Private Crownover. "Take it easy! Here have some of my orange kool aid to wash those goodies down!"

Just as he did with the food, the boy drank so deeply from Private Crownover's canteen cup that practically all of his beverage was consumed. When they finished their meal, Private Crownover gave the boy his pound cake and Private Palacios his bag of M & M candy. Then, very carefully, he opened the bag containing the pound cake, broke it into three pieces, put the smallest in his pocket along with the bag of candy and solemnly offered the other two pieces to the Marines. As a sign of thanks, the boy clasps his two hand together, gave a big smile then disappeared into the heat of the Iraqi afternoon in the direction of the town. When the Marines search the horizon for their young friend, it was as though he vanished into thin air.

Later that evening, the two Marines told their story of a young Iraqi boy who joined them for lunch earlier that day. "What are you two guys talking about? All women and children in Fallujah were evacuated days ago. Only foreign fighters are in that town," replied Gunnery Sergeant Virgil Todd.

"How do you know that Gunny?" replied Private Palacios.

" 'Cause I personally escorted them out before we attacked the town. So I'm tellin' you there were no kids in Fallujah."

"But we saw him with our own eyes, Gunny!" both Marines insisted. The two Marine Privates looked at each other then said aloud: "Do you suppose...? Naw!! It can't be!"

Faith Re-Born

For nearly two weeks everything seemed to be going wrong for 21 years old Marine Lance Corporal Shaun Cooper. So much so that even his faith was slipping away, it would seem, each and every day. Early on a hot August morning, Lance Corporal Cooper prayed: "Lord Jesus, You seem so far from me in this forsaken land I'm in right now. Lord, I've lost three of my best friends over here in Iraq. I just don't know why they had to die! They were good men! They prayed everyday. They fed, clothed and gave to drink hurting, starving and homeless Iraqis in accordance with Your Most Holy Word. Please, Lord, I humbly pray that You do something to build my faith in You. I'm so scared and weak right now and I need Your help. Amen."

That afternoon while his platoon was engaged in a mission to reduce the violence against Iraqi civilians, an Iraqi man and his wife came out of nowhere. "American, help! My daughter hurt! My daughter hurt bad! Please, American! Help me, please!"

At first, Lance Corporal Cooper thought the couple's pleas were a set up to ambush him and the members of his squad. All of that changed when he saw a little 7 or 8 year old girl laying on the ground bleeding about her head. At that instance, Lance Corporal Cooper lost all fear and suspicion for this family. He immediately radioed for a medical helicopter to come to pick up the badly injured girl and her young parents. In less than fifteen minutes, the helicopter whisked the little girl, her parents and Lance Corporal Cooper off. Arriving at a medical aid station, a physician attending the young girl examined the little girl. His prognosis was not a good one.

"The little girl's head injuries are so severe that surgery might not do anything for her. Plus, she's lost so much blood as well. I just don't know, Lance Corporal."

Now crying out loud, the little girl's parents' grief could not be contained. Lance Corporal Cooper stepped forward, "Sir, could you go ahead with the operation, please? Maybe she'll be restored."

"Very well," responded the Army surgeon. "I and my surgical team will give her our best effort. Pray we are successful. She'll need it."

From the waiting room, the little girl's parents walked up to Lance Corporal Cooper to thank him for all that he had done to save the life of their little girl.

"I'm not done," responded Lance Corporal Cooper. "Let us pray for your daughter's well being."

"We Christian!" responded the little girl's father. "We Caldean Christians. Let us pray, please!"

With clasped hands, the father, mother and Lance Corporal Cooper prayed out loud, two in Arabic, the other in English. After 12 hours of surgery, the little girl was wheeled into the recovery room. Four days passed but nothing had changed. The little girl remained in a coma.

But just outside her room, the three remained in prayer.

On the fifth day, Lance Corporal Cooper stepped forward for a second time then said, "Little girl, if you can hear me, move one of your hands." Through an Arabic speaker, very slowly and with a great deal of difficulty, the little girl moved her left wrist. Her parents, the nurses and Lance Corporal Cooper went wild. At that moment, Lance Corporal Cooper's faith soared. Lance Corporal Cooper knew, from that point, that the little girl would be okay. In three weeks following their prayers, the little girl was dismissed from the hospital with no sign of brain damage. A small surgical scar was the only evidence that she had been injured.

On the day of the little Iraqi girl's dismissal from the Army field hospital, Lance Corporal Cooper was asked by his new Iraqi friends through a translator: "Mr. American Marine does any of this mean anything to you? On the day my daughter was restored to me and her mother, I saw brightness in your face like I have never seen in any other person. It was though God had smiled upon you."

"Yes," Lance Corporal Cooper replied that he was aware of the spark of faith that had ignited in his person. "These events for me was given me to re-build my weaken faith in the Almighty God whom I began to lose faith in. Like your daughter, who was given her life back, I was given my eternal life back. Like your daughter's movement of her hand, my heart and soul was moved to understand that there is a God who is living, present and loves us all without conditions. That something as slight as the movement of a hand can be so meaningful is God's work. I'm glad to have been able to help you and your daughter, sir. Your presence saved my life—eternal life. I'm eternally grateful!"

Good Samaritan Or Onlooker: Which Are You?

Marine Sergeant Jack "Action Jackson" Thompson sat in his Battalion's makeshift chapel listening to the chaplain's sermon that discussed the "Good Samaritan. "I can't imagine passing an injured man by without trying to help that person out," said the Marine Corpsman. And sitting there in the chapel it really did seem unthinkable.

Two days after the service, Sergeant Thompson's platoon was out on a mission to protect Iraqi citizens from terrorist acts in the town of Fallujah. As his unit neared the center of the city, there was a commotion roughly a block away. Sergeant Thompson and his squad saw a man lying on the ground and chaos all around him. What looked to be an angry crowd stood over the dying man with sticks and clubs ready to end his life.

The ten man Marine squad intervened asking the crowd to move away from the man through a translator. According to the people present, the man, less than twenty minutes earlier had detonated a bomb that killed 15 women and 6 very young children.

"Help me!" plead the injured man.

At that moment every Marine rifle was trained on the man lying on the ground.

"What if we try to help and he set off a second bomb? Everyone in my squad will be killed and so will more Iraqi citizens," thought Sergeant Thompson. Suddenly Sergeant Thompson saw the top of a little book sticking out of his medical bag. It was his Bible still folded back to the chaplain's lesson of the past week service about the Good Samaritan. His righteous words barreled back to him: "I can't imagine passing an injured man by without trying to help that person out." At that point Sergeant Thompson's own hypocrisy startled him.

After a moment and a short prayer, Sergeant Thompson held up his medical bag with a white background red cross up above his head for everyone to see. "I come in peace in the Name of God!" shouted Sergeant Thompson as he made his way towards the injured man. Bending down the Corpsman took several bandages out of his bad, search for the man's injury and applied the bandages to stop the bleeding. At that point, the man went into shock. Without hesitation, Sergeant Thompson called for a helicopter. In a matter of minutes, a rescue unit carried the bomber off to a field hospital for treatment and surgery.

Although angry, the crowd, with the help of the Marine squad, cleared the area of the dead then gently placed the injured in hospital vehicles to rush off to another nearby Marine field aid station for treatment of their injuries. It was as if an Almighty Being calmed the crowd down to allow the Marines and Sergeant Thompson to come to the assistance of one who had killed and injured so many.

On his return to his base camp, Sergeant Thompson, in a thoughtful moment, felt he had not done much. But what haunted him even more was that he had come so close to doing nothing at all…only days after being so certain of himself regarding the subject of good Samaritan. As Sergeant Thompson passed the bed of the man who had killed so many, the bomber looked and smiled at Sergeant Thompson as though to say "thanks".

Sergeant Thompson later learned that the bomber he saved that hot July day in Fallujah became a Christian. Instead of bombing to killed human souls, that man began telling Iraqis of the American Marine who opened his eyes to a God of unconditional love who came to save human souls.

Marine Corpsman Sergeant Jack "Action Jackson" Thompson learned that at times God has a way of calling our bluffs as He did in his instance. He came away with an unforgettable lesson—He must show faith with action, prayer and deeds, not with theory and words.

How Blessed We Are!

"Hey, Sarge! Can I talk to you for a minute?" asked Marine Private Courtney DeShazo.

"Sure!" responded Marine Sergeant Kevin Chambers. "What do you want to talk about?"

"Sarge, I've been watching you for three weeks. I've been noticing that you pray an awful lot. Before you eat, you pray. When the First Sergeant or CO chews you out, you pray. Before you hit the sack, you pray. Why? What do you get out of it? Does God answer any of your prayers? Are you a Christian? Why do you pray that much?"

"Whoa, Private! You're asking a lot of questions! Let me try to take them one at a time. Yes, I'm a Christian. I pray for a variety of reasons. I pray for patience, to be fair to you and all the other members of our squad, to thank God for what I have, for my food, for our leaders... I could really go on for a long time, Private, because I am really blessed!"

"Would you say that God answers prayer?"

"Yes, I would! God have given me food to eat, a very good country to live in, air to breathe and much, much more!"

"But I would say, Sarge, that for every example you just gave there must be millions of unanswered prayers. By telling me things most people, we know generally have, isn't that sort of misleading people, Sarge? 'Cause there are so many out there who don't think God ever answers their prayers. They also think God doesn't like them or that something is wrong with them."

"Well, listening to what you're saying, I'll guess you or someone you know had some problems and/or disappointments that have left you or them disillusioned with God. It's pretty easy to come to the conclusion that God doesn't answer prayer when a person fights difficult problems for a long time without making any progress. When I listen to what you're saying, Private DeShazo, I think about Job. Do you know who Job was?"

"Yeah, he was the guy who I recall lost everything but didn't, in fact, refused to disown or trash God," responded Private DeShazo.

"You're exactly right. Job had every reason to feel deserted, unloved, and uncared for by God. But you know what, he didn't. He continued to pray, remain loyal and faithful to God in spite of just about everyone he knew told him (Job) to curse God and die. Job's story is so powerful to me because the whole story is an example of a test of faith. A person of no or little faith would curse God. You see, Private, I've come to realize through my reading of Job just how blessed I really am. If you can believe this, if all I had was nothing but the clothes on my back, no food and no water, I would still be blessed!"

"Man, Sarge, I didn't think about Job and the stuff he went through. But I quit believing in God because nothing seems to go right in my life. And every time I pray nothing seems to ever happen to me for the good."

"Another great example of faith and prayer was Monica, the mother of Augustine of Hippo, a fifth century AD, "Father of the Early Church", and Christian scholar. Augustine, in his youth, was engaged in the sins of alcoholism and womanizing in spite of his mother's attempts to raise him as a Christian. Monica prayed for him everyday for the rest of her life. It was only on her deathbed did Augustine renounce his sin-filled life to a Godly life. Monica prayed for Augustine for more than twenty year before his conversion

"Private! Private! Remember what I said when we first began talking about this subject, how I thanked God for what I do have? I don't deserve what I do have but I have them. So I'm thankful to God for what He has seen fit to give me. Whatever else I get in this life is a blessing. Job's story should be a memorable lesson for everyone. We should thank God daily for what He has given us. We should continue to pray and be faithful no matter how tough things get. Remember this that God is in control. He knows what you need and He will take care of everything. You've seen me praying and think I pray a lot."

"Yeah, Sarge, you sure do."

"Well, Private, I really feel as though I don't pray enough. I have missed prayer opportunities."

It has been said that God answers prayers in three ways: yes, no and wait. A person of faith should never concede to unbelief in the face of unresolved conflict. We have been told to pray without ceasing. In due time, you will realize that your faith will not be in vain.

The Greatest Day

Early on a hot July, 2005 morning in Central Iraq, Marine Sergeant Alan Brightwood sat half asleep on his bunk. "Another day," he muttered as he brushed the thick black hair out of his eyes.

"Which day do you think, Sarge, is the greatest day of your life?" Marine Lance Corporal Tanner Ford asked.

"The greatest day?" Sergeant Brightwood said. "Let me see, the day I was born. No, I don't think so. Maybe when I graduated from high school and I finally got out of school. Nah!!!" Sergeant Brightwood put his head in his cupped hands. "Hey! Why are you asking me this kind of question so darn early in the morning, Ford?"

"Because, it is a great time," the Lance Corporal replied. "This is as good as any day to ask such a question. Sarge, I think you're looking at the greatest day in your life from the wrong perspective. How 'bout the greatest day being the one you're living right now. It sure beats the alternative you gotta admit, Sarge!"

"Today?" Sergeant Brightwood said as he wiped his eyes a second time. Then he understood that Lance Corporal Ford was right. This was not just "another typical day". It, in fact was THE day, the only one that he had. It was the only day he could, in fact, actually touch reality. A day filled with possibilities—a day to grow closer to God.

Sergeant Brightwood always remembered his brief military duty with Lance Corporal Ford. For he came to conclude on the day he met the Lance Corporal was one of the greatest day of his life. It was like putting on a new freshly cleaned uniform on his humdrum, filthy existence. That day was very special. But it was not the greatest day in Sergeant Brightwood's life. No, it was this day—TODAY!

Mission Accomplishment

It was 0645, the beginning of another hectic day for Marine Captain Angelo Bridgewater as Company Commander of a Company of more than 200 marines on the move in Iraq. Captain Bridgewater's marines were making their push towards the capital city Baghdad. Lance Corporal Mona Hernandez, one of the Captain's supply personnel, watched as her Commander shuffled through piles of materials and papers left over from the day before. He desperately needed to complete and forward a report by 0700 to Battalion Headquarter but he could not locate the form on his laptop computer. Five minutes of frantic searching unearthed the form from his hard drive but the battery of his computer began warning that it was low.

"I think I'm losing my mind!" muttered the veteran officer.

Lance Corporal Hernandez, though a junior to the Captain in terms of rank and military experience, surveyed the situation then replied, "Sir, if you download notebook software authorized by the Navy, it will make efforts much more manageable, sir. It will clean up the mess you have, sir."

"Clean up the mess," thought Captain Bridgewater. "Let me have your CD, Corporal, to download that program. After e-mailing his Battalion report, Captain Bridgewater downloaded the suggested program. He began transferring key information under significant files that he could readily access. For roughly two hours, Captain Bridgewater made transfers, mergers and deletions from his computer. Soon Captain Bridgewater was able to zoom through his reports and received timely reports from his subordinate platoons by having them download the program he received from his Corporal.

Lance Corporal Hernandez's advice was a work and sanity saver for Captain Bridgewater. Years later, her words continued to influence his work effort and habits. Captain Bridgewater, now Major Bridgewater, learned to organize his work as well as his spiritual life no matter how late he must work or how tired he may become—he puts everything in place then develops a plan for the following day.

Likewise, God is not one who likes things to be disorderly in a person's daily life. Through prayer and reference to Sacred Scripture, persons CAN get their spiritual and daily lives in order. We are challenged to find our advice from places we least expect them. Only are we able to accomplish these tasks if we open our hearts and mind to them. And when we do, we benefit in every phase of life as well as please our Heavenly Father who watches from above.

Fields Of Hope And Courage

Pete Coleman loved baseball and dreamed of becoming a major league player someday. He was born in Cromwell, Oklahoma, where young boys and girls played baseball every chance they had to do so. Pete's future seemed great as he had great coaching from a father who played for several seasons with the St. Louis Cardinals in the major leagues and a mother who played softball in college for the University of Oklahoma.

As a member of a little league team, Pete's baseball skills were evident. It was difficult for pitchers to get hardly any pitch by him. In high school, Pete was a .525 hitter, had an earned run average of 0.68 with 114 home runs in 4 years. Sports writers and critics referred to Pete as the best baseball player in Oklahoma since Johnny Bench—the Baseball Hall of Fame Catcher from Bing, Oklahoma. The future appeared bright for Pete in professional baseball.

Then on September 11, 2001 two terrorist planes plowed into the twin towers. Pete could hardly contain his anger and vowed to do whatever he could to ensure such an act would not happen again. He put aside his own interest for that of a grieving nation and joined the Marines. Soon after Basic Training, Pete went to his Commanding Officer to request a tour of duty to Iraq. During the Battle for Fallujah, a foreign fighter's bullet tore through his right forearm severing it. Though his life was spared, he laid in a Navy hospital wondering if life would be worth living now that his throwing hand was gone forever. As he prayed for guidance and hope, suddenly a defiant flash of strength filled every fiber of his body. Pete vowed to become a professional baseball player in spite of his disability.

Upon his release from the Marine Corp, Pete began using his left hand. To help him, Pete obtained the services of a strength and conditioning coach. In less than a year, Pete was throwing a baseball from his left side even harder than he did when he threw using his right hand with greater accuracy. For Pete, his recovery and progress was nothing short of a miracle—a blessing from God. More good news came his way when the military decided to allow Pete to purchase a prosthetic forearm.

During a Pony League game, Pete was called on to pitch. What could it hurt thought the manager? The team was losing by a score of 14 to 1 in the 5th inning. Of the 12 batters Pete faced, he struck out 11. His outing so impressed a scout that Pete was offered a contract immediately following the game and sent to the minor leagues. After a year in the minor leagues, major league clubs rushed their scouts down to see the "one armed wonder". Pete's fastball, curve ball and slider and the speeds he threw so confused batters and put smiles on the faces of General Managers and Managers. The following spring, Pete was given his Major League opportunity with the St. Louis Cardinals—his boyhood team of choice. As a rookie pitcher, Pete had won 11 games losing only 2. It was thought Pete would have never lost if the team did not commit the three errors causing those games to be lost. Pete went on for several seasons living his dream and enjoying life in spite of the injury.

Pete Coleman could have sat back, accepted his injury and lived his life wondering about what could have been. Instead, he worked hard and with the help of God became a major league pitcher and lived his dream. Pete's story, though fictional, has a real message: He was physically handicapped, but not when it came to courage, patience and a willingness to work hard against the odds. He never lost hope. He never gave up his lifelong dream. He put his trust in God and left his circumstance in His Hands. With God in this author's corner, why should I give up? Why should you the reader give up as well?

Foolish Venture

During the Battle for Fallujah, Iraq, Lance Corporal Harlan Ducksworth was seriously injured by what appeared to be a mortar round. Fear of being physically disfigured and in pain for life, Lance Corporal Ducksworth screamed for members of his squad to end his life. Rather than honor his request, the squad leader ordered Lance Corporal Ducksworth be immediately evacuated to the nearest American Medical Aide Station where he was admitted to surgery. Following fourteen hours in surgery, Lance Corporal Ducksworth was heard to say to his fellow Marines: "Guys what I said to you was really stupid. Sorry. I was outta of my head. I've come to realize that I've said some real stupid things in the past and if I live for any length of time, it likely I'll do it again."

Those of us who have sat down to reflect upon the comings and goings of life, have more than likely heard someone or perhaps even stated words far worse than Lance Corporal Ducksworth's in critical moments of their lives. Some have cussed or cursed the very Name of God, others have made rebellious statements and other even rose to the level of disowning and rejecting the very existence of God for years as well as influence others to do the same.

In time, however, some of those who rebelled against God came to realize their mistake or mistakes. During periods of personal and social conflict and tragedy, the Name of God is invoked more often than any—respectfully and disrespectfully (Oh, God!; My, God!; Oh, my, God!). Those who have had war time battlefield experience and lived through it will tell you that nothing or no one is called upon more often than God among Christians, agnostics and even atheists. This confirms the statement: "There are no atheists on the battlefield."

It is written in Psalm 39, the Psalm of comfort, to those who are in pain and suffering often turn to. At the time he composed the Psalm, David was seriously ill and was thought to be near death. Initially, he suffered in silence. However, when he could not stand his suffering any longer, he prayed:

> *"Show me, O Lord, my life's end*
> *and the number of my days,*
> *let me know how fleeting is my life.*
> *You have made my days a mere handbreadth;*
> *the span of my years is as nothing before You.*
> *Each man's life is but a breath.*
>
> *Man is a mere phantom as he goes about life.*
> *He hustles about, but only in vain;*
> *he heaps up wealth, not knowing who will get it.*
> *But now, Lord, what do I look for?*
> *My hope is in You.*
> *Save me from all my transgressions;*
> *do not make me the scorn of fools.*
> *I was silent; I would not open my mouth,*
> *for You are the one who has done this,*
> *Remove Your scourge from me.*
> *I am overcome by the flow of Your hand.*
> *You rebuke and discipline men for their sin;*
> *You consume their wealth like a moth—*
> *each man is but a breath.*

> ***Hear my prayer, O Lord,***
> ***listen to my cry for help;***
> ***be not deaf to my cries.***
> ***I dwell with You as an alien,***
> ***a stranger, as all my fathers were.***
> ***Look away from me, that I may rejoice again***
> ***before I depart and am no more."***

As with David, the human desire for instant gratification continues to be a problem then and now. Although David's statement appears as an innocent prayer, he tells God to just leave him alone and go ahead and kill him as he (David) is just a worthless piece of "whatever".

Perhaps of all the statements in the Bible, Psalm 39 is as clear a statement of God's willingness to overlook human inconsistencies and sinful ways when He is approached with a sincere intent to reconcile with Him. It is a statement that indicates God is ready to receive anyone back at any time when one is sorry for being rebellious and stupid no matter how serious the offense is or was.

The Promise

On April 13, 2003, Marine Sergeant Tony Steward and Lance Corporal Terry Dunn, squad leader and assistant squad leader, respectively, led their squad during the Battle of Tikrit in Central Iraq. The battle went according to plan until the squad was surrounded by a larger than expected group of foreign fighters. The squad was required to seek cover in a nearby building to avoid annihilation or capture. At the end of the day, two members of the squad were injured in the fighting. One of who was Lance Corporal Dunn. As foreign fighters began massing, Sergeant Steward decided to risk his life in an effort to liberate his Marines from certain death by seeking help from higher headquarters.

Giving up ninety percent of his ammunition to his squad, Sergeant Steward ventured out under the cover of darkness to find his way to Battalion Headquarters because squad radios were damaged and rendered inoperable as the unit moved through Tikrit proper. Within ten hours of his departure, Sergeant Steward returned to the tired and hungry squad to rescue them as he had promised with a company size unit. Not one man was left behind—not even the injured Marines. The opposing forces were killed, captured or retreated.

As Jesus prepared to leave His disciples for a second time, He promised to return. He told His disciples, "If I go and prepare a place for you, I will come again and receive you to Myself; that where I am, there you may be also." Even after enduring the excruciating pain and torture of crucifixion, Jesus rose from the grave to ensure eternal life for those who would believe IN Him as their Savior by faith. This knowledge is not a leap of unsubstantiated faith, as those who hate Christ and Christianity constantly preach, but truth. Truth that is revealed by the Holy Spirit daily.

Those in Christ may rest assured that He will return to gather His own and take them to the place He has prepared for them. This is His promise for everyone is true and reliable. Jesus has always been true to His Word. This you can be assured of with or without a doubt.

Gosh Something Sure Stinks!

Navy Seaman Apprentice Curtis Jacobsen was a generous sailor. Ask him for a dollar for a can of pop or to gamble on the lottery and he would give to the person asking. When another sailor wanted to purchase a $250.00 iPod, he went to Seaman Apprentice Jacobsen who promptly gave the sailor $200. Though Seaman Apprentice Jacobsen had a serious drinking problem, no one paid him much attention. In fact, members of Seaman Apprentice Jacobsen's ship were careful to avoid him when he came aboard ship following one of his "adventures". Then one day Kristine Pattison invited him to join the ship's little prayer group that generally met once a week.

"Will you come?" Seaman Apprentice Pattison asked.

Seaman Apprentice Jacobsen hesitated, "But I can't come to a God-meeting smelling...like...like...whiskey. What would the others think of me?"

Seaman Apprentice Pattison smiled and replied, "Gosh, all of us smell of something. One of us has a problem with eating too much. Another criticizes members of their unit all of the time. And another has a problem with unforgiveness. God knows exactly how bad we all 'smell', if you will 'stink' but He still He loves us unconditionally anyhow. So won't you come? How 'bout it!"

The stunned young sailor understood. He began to laugh even while crying a little. "You bet! Ah, yes. I'll come! Are you sure I can come?"

""Sure. I'm absolutely certain," replied Seaman Apprentice Pattison. You'll see. You'll feel His presence."

"Thank you! Thank you! Thank you very much!" as he turned and walked away.

The little prayer group was uncomfortable with Seaman Apprentice Jacobsen at first. But the more members opened themselves up to their new participant; each member came to love him. Oh, Seaman Apprentice, Jacobsen still had some very tough problems to deal with and overcome. But wasn't he a great deal like the rest of us in the church family?

Navy

Navy Song

The Lottman-Savino version published around 1950 in London by Francis, Day & Hunter is:

Verse 1

> Anchors Aweigh, my boys
> Anchors Aweigh
> Farewell to college joys
> We sail at break of day, day, day, day
> Through our last night ashore
> Drink to the foam
> Until we meet once more
> Here's wishing you a happy voyage home!

Bridge

> Heave a ho there! sailor
> Ev'rybody drink up while you may
> Heave a ho there! sailor
> For you're gonna sail at break of day
> Drink a-way, Drink a-way,
> For you sail at break of day, Hey!

Verse 2

Stand Navy, down the field, sails set to the sky.
We'll never change our course, so Army you steer shy-y-y-y.
Roll up the score, Navy, Anchors Aweigh
Sail, Navy, down the field and sink the Army, sink the Army Grey

I Am With You

Petty Officer Melda Ferguson was having a very, very bad day and was in an equally bad mood as she drove to the base commissary to pick up additional food. "Oh, Lord Jesus," she said in despair, "Where are You? I don't know what's wrong with me today. Everything and everybody I've been around has been an utter disaster. I feel as though I'm going to lose my mind, Lord. Please, Lord, if You could just touch me in some way even if it is for a brief moment and lift my dreadful spirit. Help me!"

At that time, Petty Officer Ferguson turned on the radio. And what occurred appeared to be heaven sent. She heard the soft strains of the "Our Father". It filled the car. Then a voice read Scripture. Moving over to the side of the road and away from traffic, she began to cry softly. Not tears of sadness, but tears of gratitude. "God had heard my prayer and touched me through this radio broadcast."

Not realizing that she had even started her car, she found herself at the base commissary parking lot. Although she knew where she was, she just sat in her car. The hymns and soothing voice of the radio commentator continued to minister to her. "I really don't want to leave this car. I feel Your presence, Lord," she said, "In the commissary; everyone is caught up with making food and other item purchases for themselves or their families. They are not thinking of You. They may even be visiting with each other. I don't want to be around people if I can't be with You. Lord, may I just sit here for the rest of the day in this parking lot? This is so wonderful!"

It was just at that moment that the announcer quoted Jesus' saying, "I am with you always". It was at that point Petty Officer Ferguson knew she had to leave her car. She heard no voice but what appeared to be an internalized force seemed to say, "Go right now into the commissary and take Me with you. Go in with a smile on your face and love in your heart. Be kind and cheerful to everyone you meet and talk to for I will be in you and with you."

Looking For The Good

"Dumb, stupid, idiotic Marine!" remarked Chief Petty Officer Terry Butler as a small compact car splashed muddy water on his just cleaned and pressed white uniform. "Marines always drive like they're trying to get to a beer party. They never consider the other guy! As he boarded the ship ordered to the Middle East, he learned differently. The offending driver turned out to be the ship's and Petty Officer Butler's Captain, a twenty-five year Navy man!

The above incident is a reminder of how often we all are guilty of making generalizations. To assume something is so because someone is female or male, young or old, black or white, learned or not so intelligent is sloppy thinking at best, down right ignorance at worst. The Bible is full of examples of such human indiscretions that demonstrate the consequence of prejudicial thinking.

If you recall, Jonah did not want to go to Nineveh because he looked down upon its citizens as unworthy of his person. In John, Philip's friend Nathaniel, in a less than palatable condescending manner, remarked about Jesus, "Can there be any good thing come out of Nazareth?" Philip's response to the statement was, "Come and see for yourself."

It is Christlike to look for the good in others, not the bad or wicked. If a person says they are a follower of the Master but consistently makes or has negative comments about people or a person that cannot be support, he or she is not following Christ's command to love as He loves each one individually regardless of their condition or station in life. Unconditional love is kind, understanding, forgiving with no strings attached. Dispense with love this very day in all that you say and do not just towards the one you like but those you do not like or may be in conflict with. The likelihood is you will receive unconditional love in return perhaps in abundance!

The Important Things

After completing the expansion bridge across Baghdad, Navy Lieutenant Edgar Evans spoke out. Too much time and energy was being spent worrying about the grand structures of this city and not enough time caring for those who have to live here.

"Roads, airports and store fronts are important. In addition to all of these things, we've got to be doing the Lord's work here in Baghdad. If we are to serve Him fully, we'll see, eventually, that He'll take care of the small stuff.

"I know this is an Islamic country," Lieutenant Evans continued. "Instead of being concerned about what religion they are and the fact they were our enemies, we should get simple little food baskets together. I'll bet the every day, common Iraqi won't care who they got the food from. I prefer it be us though. But I really think they will appreciate it—a lot!"

When Lieutenant Evans was finished, his commanding officer, Commander Jason Lee thought his junior officer mighty naïve to think that God would step in to take care of the needs of the United States Navy and re-build Baghdad city. But his idea received the enthusiastic support of the Admirals and General officers within his command structure.

A week before Christmas, the Navy came through. There were over two thousand baskets of food. Food, many had not eaten for many years during the Saddam Hussein era. And in each basket was a leg of lamb.

After the Christmas season, the American armed services command noticed the cooperation of the citizens of that Baghdad community had grown. Word of what the American military had done spread around the community. Soon generous Americans military personnel of the armed services re-built their local electric grids, bridges and buildings. But local citizens of Baghdad, more than these works, mentioned the food baskets they had received. Men, women and children came forward to remove ruble to help Americans with the rebuilding of their community. Despite what news outlets had reported, peace and cooperation reigned in this Baghdad community. Structures, in some areas, never seen before were put in place with little or no conflict from the local population.

Lieutenant Evans was right in his thinking. The Lord shelters those who earnestly believe only in Him and who will submit to serve Him unconditionally.

In Due Time

"Say doc do you have anything for headaches? I've got a splitter," complained Petty Officer Tim Morrison.

"Yeah, I've got something for a headache," responded the ship's physician.

"I hope its strong, doc! I've had one headache after another."

"Sure, not a problem."

After an examination and taking Petty Officer Morrison vitals, the ship doctor asked him a question. "Petty Officer," he began, "you may choose not to answer my question, but I'm going to ask it anyhow. Do you have some deep resentments or hatreds in your life?" Initially, the sailor denied that he had any such feelings. Then he admitted that had some anxious moments for about ten days or so. Another man had been promoted ahead of him during the ship's mission in the Persian Gulf roughly a month ago.

"I should have gotten that promotion. Everybody knows I do the best work in the ship's engine room. Since he was promoted, I haven't talked to him because I really get angry when I run into him."

"Your headaches could be related," the doctor told him. "And even if it isn't, you are carrying some potentially destructive seeds. Why don't you discuss your problem with this fellow to God? After all from what you've told me, he has done nothing to offend you. Promotions go before a promotion board. They do the selection of a person for promotion. It is not the person who you are taking it out on.

Petty Officer Morrison took the doctor's advice, went before God to ask for forgiveness. He then went a step further to reconcile himself with the man he had known for many years but was promoted ahead of him. He confided in him the problem he had with him and asked for his forgiveness. The man was shocked but forgave him as soon as he made mention of it to him. The two men became immediate friends again. Not surprising, Petty Officer Morrison's severe headaches went away and he was able to do his work more effectively. Petty Officer Morrison was considered for promotion a year later and, in fact, was promoted.

The Conquest

Navy Petty Officer Robert Newton knew should never say "Oh, God" unless he really meant to be talking to God in prayer or doing so in a respectful manner. However, being aboard ship hundreds of sailors who made reference to the Almighty in this and a variety of other inappropriate expressive ways made it difficult for him to catch himself saying "Oh, God". Petty Officer Newton realized he needed a strategy in order to avoid taking God's Name in vain. "Oh, no!" "Oh, shoot!" "Oh, darn it" seemed more appropriate alternatives. So he would do this only to fail during moments of stress and strain.

Two hours following his prayful encounter it happened. When a subordinate left a fuel container dangerously close to an engine system, it came out. He realized he said "Oh, God" in horror. It was at that point Petty Officer Newton discovered a new way of making amends to the Lord for bad behavioral outbursts. His exclamation, "Oh, God" became the beginning of a spontaneous prayer. After "Oh, God" he would say "please help me not to lose my head in stressful moments and to praise Your Most Holy Name all the days of my life. Forgive me of my sin and sins. This I pray my most merciful and compassionate Father. Amen."

What surprised Petty Officer Newton about his new technique was that when he let an "Oh,

God" slip out; it was during those times of anger, fear, surprise and frustration. He also learned was a time to call on God for His assistance and help. In the coming weeks, he was able to overcome what was once a bad habit to be used as a reminder of Whom he needed to turn to in his weaker moments.

Being A Blessed Receiver

Like many people Navy Ensign Sharon Ramsey had been taught as a child: "It is more blessed to give than to receive". As newly commissioned officer in the United States Navy, Ensign Ramsey attempted to make this her motto no matter what her rank would become as she planned to make the Navy her career. However, she quickly learned that receiving can be a blessing as well.

While on her first tour of duty in the Persian Gulf, Ensign Ramsey became sick. So sick, in fact, that she was ordered by the ship's physician to sick bay. Reluctantly, she remained there for a week. Though fit to be returned to duty, the young Ensign had difficulty performing the simplest task. When peers or subordinates offered help, she would proudly say, "Thanks, but no."

Finally, Ensign Juanita Flores showed up to her cabin with a small container of chicken tortilla soup insisting that she take it. The two young officers chatted for roughly twenty minutes until Ensign Flores stood up then said, "Let me do some of your tasks. I can see that you are still weak from your recent illness. Before I came to your cabin, I discussed you with the Captain. He said I could help you out as long as it did not interfere with my job."

"Absolutely not," Ensign Ramsey said.

"Listen Ensign Ramsey," Ensign Flores said to her, "its not easy to be a receiver, I know, but give me the opportunity to be a giver. Don't you think it's a good idea for you to let God bless me with blessing of being one? I'm not asking for your soul or anything like that! How about it? Okay."

Ensign Flores was right! A giver needs a receiver. Will you be a Godly one should the need arise?

Christian Or Not

The simple fact is: many people who call themselves Christians do not know Christ, do not live a Christian life nor do they have the slightest idea as to what it means to live a life of faith in Christ. Navy Chaplain Robert DesJean discovered this as he and his crew set sail from Norfolk Naval Base, Virginia to serve in the Persian Gulf area.

On the way to his first duty at sea, Chaplain DesJean's ship encountered heavy, turbulent seas. Chaplain DesJean was filled with fear which he expressed to the ship's Executive Officer. The young officer stood straight and seemed oblivious to the ship's up and down, side to side movements to the stormy weather.

"Aren't you afraid," Chaplain DesJean asked her.

"No, I know the Lord Jesus Christ. He promised He'd be with me always no matter the circumstance or situation. Do you know Him?"

For the first time in his twenty-two years as a Christian minister, Chaplain DesJean realized he did not really know Christ as his personal Savior.

Many people have posed as an intimate friend of Christ and nothing refute their claim until their life was challenged with a troubling situation. That is when their true relationship with God is verified or denied—when dark clouds and uncertainty are present and our life threatened.

Throughout the two thousand years plus of the Christian era, countless stories of children, men and women are told of those who faced spiritual threatening challenges to their faith. We also more often told of the bravery of those who gave their lives as witnesses (martyrs) to their faith. Seldom are we told of those whose weakness caused them to deny Christ and a relationship with Him. However, for every martyr who died in faith, it is estimated that two to three persons denied knowing Christ in order to live and walk away from their faith because of the challenges they faced.

One of the most memorable incidents in the Bible occurred when the Israelites stood on the plain of Moab as they were about to enter the land promised them by God. Moses realized the majority of the people still questioned his leadership and God's promise in spite of what they had been through and witnessed said: "Behold, the Lord your God has set the land before you: go possess it, as the Lord God of your fathers has said to you, fear not nor be discouraged." (Deut. 1:21)

When you feel fearful or overwhelmed by circumstances that are outside your ability to control, call on the God of your Christian faith. He will always respond—of that you can be absolutely sure of!

Prayer Warrior

"Hey, Petty Officer Fields would you please pray for my little brother back home? He's going to have an operation on his hand. Could you pray that his surgery be uncomplicated and his recovery a quick one?"

"Petty Officer, my parents are talking about a divorce. They've been married more than thirty-six years. Would you please pray that they will be able to successfully work through their differences?"

"Petty Officer, I don't feel so good today. I think I have the flu. Would you pray for me to get better? I just can't take any time off my job her on the ship. Thanks Petty Officer!"

Petty Officer Michelle Fields, a mechanics specialist, learned quickly that having signed up to be one of the chaplain's prayer warriors was almost as time consuming as her ship related duties. Within one week of accepting this assignment, she found herself flooded with more than two dozen prayer requests—sailors struggling with being separated from their children or spouses; sea sickness; wondering if there is a God; a toothache to name a few. During quicker, less stressful moments of the day, Petty Officer Fields was embarrassed to admit to the chaplain that she was fed up with being a prayer warrior.

"Chaplain, I really don't have the time to pray for all of these people. This is a huge task."

"You're right Petty Officer Fields. Trust God. God knew exactly what He was doing when He chose you for this task. You'll do just fine!"

As she considered the chaplain's words, Petty Officer Fields unenthusiastically went to her quarters then went through her list of prayer requests. "Lord, King of the universe, I pray you remember…" It was at this moment that Petty Officer Fields began to understand why it was important for her to pray to the Lord for her shipmates and their petitions to God. She came to realize that as a prayer warrior she was given an opportunity for quiet time to be alone in the presence of God. Petty Officer Fields felt the obligations to others helped her see that God used her prayer warrior position as a way to call her back to herself in a new way. She learned to be attentive, compassionate, loving, caring and understanding to the needs of others. After being a prayer warrior, Petty Officer Fields began to wonder if this additional duty assignment was just God's way bring her closer to Him. When she thought about, God is really behind every prayer request.

So when she felt overwhelmed by all of the prayer requests, she recalled the day she felt overwhelmed with them. "Perhaps its God's way of saying, Michelle, let's talk! Time to pray!"

Hanging In There

Any Delaney, 22 years old, had become an Ensign in the United States Navy 14 months earlier. After her initial officer training, Ensign Delaney was ready to serve her nation in any manner for the greater good. While on duty in the Persian Gulf, she became gravely ill. She was in sickbay for three days before the ship's decided doctor to send her to a military hospital in Germany for additional medical care. While in Germany, Ensign Delaney reached her lowest point when it became clear to her that she was going through not one battle, but two. One battle was a battle of physical pain that the medical profession could not determine the reason or reasons for, and the other with self-pity.

"Chaplain, I'm almost at the end of my rope. In all of my life, I've never suffered like this ever! I've known good health with just an occasional cold once in a while. I've had doctors check me and check me. I've had nurses poke me and poke me to draw blood and they still can't tell me what's wrong. They're telling me that they are planning to send me home for further observation and testing. I don't think I can take much more of this, chaplain!"

"Well, Ensign, you know what you can do at this point don't you?"

"No, I don't."

Taking a brown handkerchief out of his pocket then tying a knot in it, the chaplain said. "I'll tie a knot in this handkerchief as a symbol to you as a way of saying 'hang on'. When everything else seems to fail you, look to God and hold onto Him for your answer. He'll pull you through like nothing else will. I'm also suggesting you place your trust in Him. That is why I'm giving you this handkerchief in a knot."

The chaplain's words were like medicine to Ensign Delaney's spirit. At the time, Ensign Delaney felt her future in the Navy looked bleak; her health seemed uncertain, even intolerable, if she thought of it in terms of days and weeks. But if she could just find a way to hang on, maybe she would get better.

Once the chaplain left her, Ensign Delaney asked the nurse to get her three more handkerchiefs. She took the handkerchiefs, tied them onto the one she was given by the chaplain and hung it onto the railing of her hospital bed. When the pain came or when self-pity took over, Ensign Delaney would grab hold and say to herself, "In the Name of the Lord Jesus Christ, I can work through this whatever this is that causing me my problem. I know You are me, Oh God! You are my refuge and my strength." And holding on just five to ten minutes at a time did wonders for Ensign Delaney. Although the best doctors in the military and from civilian medical institutions could not diagnosis Ensign Delaney's illness and pain, she miraculously came through her mysterious illness and pain in 33 days following its onset.

The notion of using a symbol in this manner at first appears odd, but it is not. Throughout the history of humankind and Christian history, symbols have played powerful roles. Most Americans have a sense of pride when they see the Stars and Stripes flying over a public building. The majority of Christians feel a sense of triumph from the most significant and magnificent of all human symbols—the Cross!

His Plan For You

Little did Navy Lieutenant Commander Elena Pena know, when she asked the Lord to use her, that He would put her to work performing fifteen very complicated surgeries on fifteen badly injured marines and sailors—all in the month of September. In addition to these surgeries, Commander Pena performed nearly three times that many complicated and routine surgeries on Iraqi citizens. Many of the Iraqis who Commander Pena performed surgery on had never seen a doctor and therefore their surgeries were especially difficult for her. In the opinion of both military and Iraqi civilians, Commander Pena was a bright, very competent and very loving medical doctor. She would love the babies, comfort the children, and be respectfully to every adult she would visit. If the operation didn't go right, Commander Pena would comfort the family and friends, shed a tear, and pray to her Lord for strength and guidance for any future surgeries.

When she received this unusual number of patients, Commander Pena said to a friend, an associate physician, "I'm not complaining. It's just that I'm not sure I'll have the energy to do everyone justice. I'm so afraid I'll make bad surgical mistakes if I keep this up.

While walking down a hallway following her most recent surgery, Commander Pena met another professional associate, Lieutenant

Commander Robert Prieto, a psychiatrist. Commander Prieto spent many hours each week praying with and counseling troubled service members, mainly Christian, but also non-Christians. So Commander Pena asked him, "How on God's green earth do you keep on top of all of it without going crazy? What's your secret Commander?"

Commander Prieto told her, "I just keep reminding myself, several times a day that since the Lord gave me all of this work to do. He will see me through every bit of it." Then Commander Prieto pulled a subdued Bible out of his pocket. He quickly turned the pages until he came to a passage in the Book of Job. "There's a passage in Job that really helps me every time I think I'm going to be overwhelmed. It's 'He performs the thing that is appointed for me'. Each morning when I get up out of my bunk, and while I'm brushing my teeth, walking to this hospital especially; and as I counsel a service member, regarding of the Armed Service, I repeat those words, trusting Him, every second, every minute, every hour, to do His work, not my work, but His through me. And you know what He does!!! He's never failed me! Not even once! Isn't that remarkable!"

Within minutes of talking to Commander Prieto, Commander Pena received a call over the public address system to rush to another surgery. Following the surgery, Commander Pena went to comfort the service member then went to see the chaplain for one of the little subdued green covered Bibles to carry with her. She began using the affirmation from Job every day. She no longer felt unsure nor did she lack energy. She felt confident that the Lord would carry her through the work given her. And He did. Since Commander Pena took on her new found exercise, she has not fail nor did she feel as though she feel she had failed to do His work. Now Commander Pena, when she talks to her patients she takes out her Bible then tells them of God's Plan for them. The feedback Commander Pena has received in 100% success—no failure from anyone!

God's plan can help you to know—really know what it is you are to do. You will NOT have to find yourself. And He will help you to complete it from start to its completion!

Proper Thanks

"Thank goodness we finally arrived!" said Petty Officer Melvin Conway as their ship docked in Basra, Iraq after the ship experienced waves said to be 40 or 50 feet high while in the Persian Gulf.

"What's goodness got to do with anything?" asked Petty Barbara Hinton as the anchor lowered into the bright blue waters. "C'mon! Let's give credit where credit is due Petty Officer Conway! Thank God we're here safely and live to tell another day!"

Because so many people readily spurt out, "Thank God" without doing honor to the Lord, it, more often than not, is taking God's Name in vain. However, in this instance, Petty Officer Hinton was correct when she corrected her shipmate, Petty Officer Conway.

As C.S. Lewis once remarked, "To thank goodness isn't theologically sound and ignores the One who is responsible for seeing humanity through difficulties as well as giving humanity so many things they never deserve."

The grace of God cannot be earned. It is His freed, loving gift available to anyone who, by faith, will believe in Him and accept Him without reservation. Having a great number of family and friends, thank God! Being in good health, thank God! Being free to pursue happiness, being alive and being able to go where we wish, thank God! Human, or their so-called innate goodness, could never secure a single needed or desired item for anyone at anytime were it not for Someone much bigger and more generous. Let humanity remember and acknowledge the Source of all that is good and right!

Best Counselor In The Navy

Navy Chaplain George Littlethunder from Coweta, Oklahoma was on his fourth deployment to Iraq. What was interesting about Chaplain Littlethunder was his cheerful, fatherly and easy going approach to his ministry among the crew. It did not matter who he was around. Within a matter of, say 10 minutes, those who encountered the chaplain walked away feeling good about themselves and their circumstance.

On a particularly difficult afternoon for the ship's Captain, getting away to see Chaplain Littlethunder was the best part of his afternoon away from the rigors of command—even if it was for about 20 minutes.

"Down in Oklahoma," Chaplain LIttlethunder told the Captain, "some Native American people say that if you capture and cage a coyote, another coyote will come along and feed the captured on a poisoned piece of meat to put it out of its misery. Do you believe this to be so, Captain?"

"I don't know anything at all about coyotes, their habits or really what they do insofar as their behavior. I'd say 'no' though," responded the Captain.

"Well, this is what the old people tell us. But I sure know of a few people who poison themselves and others on a consistent, steady diet of laced Kool Aid that is poison. Kool Aid laced with Anger, Hatred, Jealousy, Self-doubt with a whole lot of

Self-pity. They keep these poison locked up in themselves. Those people are so very good at giving this poison to others who willingly spread it to others they know or do not know.

"Do you think that they can be helped, chaplain?"

"Sometimes they can be helped. Sometimes not. The toughest are the ones who claim they've tried everything or the ones who blame others or God. The ones who blame others or God, I've found, refuse to take responsibility for what it is they're doing. They have nowhere to turn to."

"I'm curious, chaplain. What do you say to such people?"

"I generally say to them 'Stop trying'. Or stop looking for someone else to blame. Own up to you what you've done. They are great currents of love, forgiveness and healing flowing throughout this universe. You're the hold-up. You're blocking them with all of your gloom despair and arrogance (pride). Go home. Stay calm. Don't do anything for a little bit of time. Get out of your own way. And most of all get out of God's way. Then wait—and listen to God. God is just waiting in the wings to straighten out what you've messed up."

"And does it work?"

"Actually, more often than you might think, Captain. And when they listen to what the Creator tells them, they run around telling people I straightened things out or made a difference in their lives. But you and I know that it isn't about what I did but rather what they did with a whole lot of help from a much higher power!"

Service Members And Veterans:
A Prayer

Almighty, Omnipotent, Wise Father of humanity—

We thank You for all who are and have served in the armed services of this country. We thank You for the freedom, liberties, rights and privileges their unselfish sacrifice has earned and guarded for us over the years.
Help us to prize this freedom, these liberties, rights and privileges.
Help us to use them well and responsibly.
We ask You, O Lord, to bless every active service member and living veteran in a unique and special way this and every day of their lives as well as their family and friends.
Give special talents to those who provide service members with treatment and care.
Place in the hearts and minds of all humanity a universal desire for peace so that a day will come when all live in freedom from avarice the root cause of war.
Help us to live this and every day forward in anticipation of that blessed day when all peoples and nations live in peace with no need to possess armed forces. I/We pray in Jesus' Name. Amen.

Autobiography
Of
Stephen A. Peterson

Stephen A. Peterson, a member of the Seminole Nation of Indians, is currently employed in Oklahoma City, Oklahoma as a counseling psychologist/therapist primarily working with teenage and young adult clients. He is the author of a number of books, articles and short stories on Christianity, adolescent psychology, and issues pertaining to death and dying. He has degrees in Biological Anthropology and Psychology and has done some college teaching.

CPSIA information can be obtained
at www.ICGtesting.com
Printed in the USA
FSOW01n1233190516
20624FS

9 781438 985688